JAMES HENEGHAN

The Mystery of the GOLD RING

Cover by
Janet Wilson

Scholastic Canada Ltd.

Scholastic Canada Ltd.
123 Newkirk Road, Richmond Hill, Ontario, Canada L4C 3G5

Scholastic Inc.
555 Broadway, New York, NY 10012 USA

Ashton Scholastic Limited
Private Bag 94407, Greenmount, Auckland, New Zealand

Scholastic Australia Pty Limited
PO Box 579, Gosford, NSW 2250, Australia

Scholastic Publications Ltd.
Villiers House, Clarendon Avenue, Leamington Spa
Warwickshire CV32 5PR, UK

Canadian Cataloguing in Publication Data

Heneghan, James, 1930-
    The mystery of the gold ring

ISBN 0-590-24623-2

I. Title.

PS8565.E5854M9 1995   jC813'.54   C95-931113-0
PZL.E4My 1995

6 5 4 3 2 1   Printed in Canada   5 6 7 8/9

Manufactured by Webcom Limited

The O'Brien Detective Agency Series:

The Case of the Marmalade Cat
The Trail of the Chocolate Thief
The Mystery of the Gold Ring

Other Scholastic books by James Heneghan:

Blue

Goodbye, Carlton High
(with Bruce McBay, as "B.J. Bond")

For Samuel Douglas Peetoom Heersink.

 # Chapter 1

The three members of the O'Brien Detective Agency stared through the glass at the gold ring.

The ring was in an exhibit case in the Athens Museum. A sign on the case said, "Gold Ring of the Minotaur" in several different languages.

"It's ugly," said Clarice O'Brien.

Sadie Stewart pushed her long brown hair out of her eyes. "No it's not, Clarice. It's beautiful!"

"What's the carving on it?" said Brick, fascinated, peering into the case with wide eyes.

"A monster," said Sadie, "half man, half bull. It's called the Minotaur." She took off her glasses and polished them with a small square of cloth she always carried with her for that purpose. Sadie was a year younger than Clarice and Brick, but because she was always reading, she knew an incredible lot of stuff.

"I see nothing beautiful about a ring with a monster on it," said Clarice, fanning her flushed face rapidly with her white cotton hat. "The ring is downright creepy, if you ask me."

The museum's air conditioner didn't seem to be working. Clarice's thick red hair was sticking to the back of her neck.

The three detectives, Clarice, Sadie and Brick, were in the final two days of their two-week holiday in Athens with Sadie's parents. They could see Mr. and Mrs. Stewart over on the other side of the museum gallery, gazing up at tall marble statues of gods and goddesses. Mrs. Stewart, slim and cool in white shirt and shorts, sandals and white sunhat, was peering through her glasses at a marble likeness of Apollo, the sun god. Mr. Stewart, a plump, perspiring, cheerful man, was smiling fondly at his wife. His khaki shorts ballooned about his calves like a tent; with his Tilley hat and binoculars he looked like a tourist on the Serengeti.

"It isn't the ring that's creepy," said Sadie,

"it's you, Clarice. You just don't believe there could be a man who's half — "

"Half animal!" murmured Brick, his attention still captivated by the gold ring. "Half human, half animal!"

Clarice lifted her chin to fan her throat. "I'm ready for an ice cream, half strawberry, half chocolate. This heat — "

Her words were cut short by a sudden burst of chattering from a group of kids making their way down the gallery toward them, as noisy as birds at sunset.

Clarice groaned. "Oh, no! It's those loopy Lakers again!"

The Lakers were a school band from the Erin Lake Junior High School in Ontario. They were travelling around Greece, sightseeing and playing to anyone crazy enough, in Clarice's opinion, to listen to them. The three detectives had already met up with them at Delphi and at Olympia, where the school band had played several noisy marches in the famous original Olympic Stadium, causing music-loving tourists to make a frantic dash for the exit. Now here they were again, in Athens.

The two teachers in charge of the Lakers, a

tall, skinny man and a tiny, plump woman, followed behind their students like a pair of mismatched geese shepherding noisy, unruly goslings.

The Lakers crowded around the three detectives at the exhibit case. One boy, a wiry eighth grader with a shock of black hair that stood up from his head like a paintbrush, said, "Miss Plum, why are all those old bones in the same case as the jewellery?"

Miss Plum consulted her catalogue. "Everything you see in the glass case was found in the grave with the bones, thought to be those of the hero Theseus. There's gold, jewels, ivory combs, jewelled slippers, two jewelled daggers bearing the royal crest of the House of Athens, and the gold ring of the Minotaur." She had a calm, musical voice.

The same boy said, "Mini-tour, Miss Plum? Sounds like a short, quick trip on a Greek bus."

Everyone laughed. Miss Plum smiled. "Very funny, Kerry."

"Dead bones!" Clarice shivered in the museum's hot gallery. She turned to Sadie, "What did the Minotaur monster do?" She had to raise her voice a little because of the excited noise the Lakers were making over the bones in the exhibit case.

"He ate teenagers," said Sadie.

"He ate *what?*"

"I'll tell you later."

The man teacher leaned down over Miss Plum's shoulder to see her catalogue. His face was very close to hers. Miss Plum blushed. The man read aloud from the catalogue. "The ring of the Minotaur is believed to have supernatural powers."

"What do you think that means?" said Clarice to Sadie.

"Mr. Pollon likes Miss Plum," said Kerry, the smart-alecky boy with the black paintbrush hair, turning to answer Clarice's question before Sadie could speak. "And she likes him." He grinned at Clarice. "That's what it means."

Clarice glared at him. Kerry shrugged and turned away.

"What was all that stuff about supernatural powers, Sadie?"

"It means if you wear the ring," said Sadie, "then you become superhuman, very strong and fast, like the hero Theseus."

"Hmmph!" said Clarice.

"If you could choose something from this cabinet," Miss Plum was saying brightly to the Lakers, "what would it be? The gold ring? The jewelled slippers? A jewelled dagger, perhaps?"

Everyone began speaking at once. Most wanted the ring. One tall, willowy girl who was standing with her hands clasped together behind her sunhat, posing like the marble statue of Terpsichore over on the other side of the gallery, wanted the gold ring to help her become a famous dancer. Another girl wanted the beautiful slippers, to give to her father who always walked around at home in his socks. A boy who looked to be about fourteen wanted all the gold in the case, so he could take an early retirement and never have to go to school again.

Mr. Pollon laughed. Miss Plum smiled.

They moved to the next exhibit. The detectives moved along with them. Sadie looked at her watch. "It's four-thirty, and the museum closes at five."

"I've had enough," said Clarice. She nodded her head decisively. "I'm tired of old dead things."

Sadie's eyes widened behind her glasses.

"How can you say that, Clarice! There's so much here! Just think, all this stuff dug up from graves thousands of years old! It's mind-boggling!"

"It doesn't boggle my mind, it just gives me the shivers," said Clarice. "How would you like someone to dig up *your* grave a thousand years from now and have someone poke at your bones! Or have someone say, 'These funny objects on Sadie Stewart's face were called glasses!' You wouldn't like it one bit!"

"But don't you feel a sense of wonder, Clarice? We're actually in Athens, the ancient playround of the gods!" Sadie's voice was hushed with awe. "Athens, city of myth!"

Clarice said, "Myths are just stories, everyone knows that."

"Don't you be so sure," said Sadic. "This Agora is full of the spirits of ancient Greece."

"What does Agora mean again?" said Clarice.

Sadie put on her "allow me to explain" expression, which involved an upward tilting of the chin and a pursing of the lips. "It means Gathering Place. This whole area, including the museum and Vulcan's Temple, was a big marketplace with graves and shrines and shops and cafés and offices, and was always crowded with people. Just like Granville Island back home, only bigger."

Brick's mind seemed to be still on the Minotaur. "Half animal," he muttered to himself.

Tall and thin, with spiky yellow hair, a freckled, tawny complexion and unblinking amber eyes, he rarely spoke. Brick's main usefulness as a detective was his astonishing athletic ability; when it came to climbing rooftops and squeezing through windows he was worth his weight in french fries.

Miss Plum was now standing beside a huge jar. "This is called an amphora," she said, "used for storing water, and it's over two thousand years old, imagine that!"

When the group had moved on, Sadie stood on her tiptoes trying to see into the jar. "Runaway slaves sometimes hid in these jars and scratched their names on the inside," she said. She pulled a book of myths from her hip pocket and handed it to Clarice. "Hold this." Sadie always carried a book. "Give me a leg up," she said to Brick.

Brick made a cradle of his hands and heaved Sadie up onto the rim of the jar. Sadie rolled over the smooth lip, and disappeared inside with a thump and a splash.

"Sadie!" said Clarice. "Are you all right?"

Clarice and Brick stood on the tips of their toes and peered into the jar.

Sadie's voice boomed out. "It's dark in here!" She grasped the rim of the jar and tried to pull herself out. "And it's wet! Help me!"

Clarice and Brick took her by the wrists and pulled.

"Ouch!" yelled Sadie. "Take it easy!"

The jar tilted.

"Stop it!" yelled Sadie.

The jar righted itself.

"What you do, you children?" It was a security guard. He looked down into the jar and saw Sadie. "Wait!" He went away and was back in seconds with a small stepladder. He chewed his black mustache angrily as he climbed up the ladder. Reaching down, he grasped Sadie by the elbows, lifted her up and out of the jar, and lowered her to the floor.

Sadie's legs and sandals were soaked. A puddle began to form on the floor about her feet. She jerked a thumb angrily at the jar. "What's the big idea!" she said to the guard. "A person could drown in that thing! I could sue you."

The guard glared at Sadie. He pointed to the exit. "You leave!" He turned and glared at Clarice and Brick. "Out!"

The three friends started for the exit. Sadie's feet squelched on the polished floor. She said to Clarice, "Just because it's a water jar doesn't mean it should be full of water!"

Clarice took her arm. "Calm down, Sadie, it wasn't *full* of water, there was only a few centimetres. They probably had the thing outside in the rain. No harm done. Your sandals will soon dry in the sun."

They passed Sadie's mom and dad. "We're going back to the hotel," said Sadie.

"Your feet are wet," said Mrs. Stewart, staring at Sadie's sandals.

"I had an accident."

"You shouldn't leave it for so long, dear," said Mrs. Stewart. She sighed. "We'll see you back at the hotel."

They walked back down the gallery through the pottery section and through the display of bronze cremation urns. The guard, hands on hips, watched them go. It was almost closing time. The other guards were consulting their watches; people were starting to leave. As they passed by the Theseus exhibit the three sleuths saw a small group of Lakers still gathered about the glass case: Kerry was bent over, hands on knees; the girl who wanted to be a dancer leaned her slim elbows on top of the case; two others, a girl with a wild mop of dark curly hair and a slim, good-looking boy, stood with their heads close together.

They all looked to be eighth graders.

And they were all staring with greedy eyes at the gold ring of the Minotaur.

 **Chapter 2**

Sadie said, "Being thrown out of a museum is so embarrassing."

The three friends walked back to their hotel, which was just a short distance from the museum, on the other side of the Agora fence. They were tired. Their day had started when the sun was barely up with a visit to the Acropolis, and now their legs ached from all the walking they had done.

Clarice said, "Did you see all those kids staring like a bunch of crazies at the gold ring? How can they believe all that supernatural junk? It's only a ring!"

Sadie, still smarting from their undignified

ejection from the museum, said scornfully, "You're dead wrong, Clarice. It's not *only* a ring, it's a national treasure. And I believe it really does have supernatural powers."

"Hmmph!" said Clarice.

"Hmmph yourself!" said Sadie.

"Half human — " Brick murmured to himself.

They trooped into the Ariadne Hotel.

"People who believe in supernatural powers," declared Clarice, "have to have their shoelaces tied for them."

They plodded up the stairs. The Ariadne had no elevator. Sadie's parents preferred old, "colourful" hotels.

"You've got no imagination, that's your problem, Clarice," said Sadie. "It's like you had a lobotomy of the imagination. Life is full of magic. You just can't see it, that's all."

"Somebody should do you a favour and give you a bottomy of the tongue," said Clarice. "You talk too much."

"The word is lob— "

"Shut up, Sadie! That's an order!" Clarice pushed the key into the lock. The door swung open.

"We're not on a case, Clarice," objected Sadie. "You can't give orders when we're not on a case."

"I wish we *were* on a case," said Clarice. "I'm fed up with suffocating heat, and ruins, and museums with marble statues and bronze cremation urns. I'd give anything for an ice-cold Slurpee and an interesting case to solve. I can't wait to get home. I bet the cases have piled up since we left, a dozen crimes maybe, and everyone waiting for us to come back and solve them."

"Well, that's showing appreciation, I must say," said Sadie angrily. "My mom and dad are kind enough to bring you to Greece, and all you can say is — "

"If I'd known that all we'd be doing is looking at dead bones and dragging ourselves around musty old museums every day I would've — "

"Would've what? Been bored to death in Vancouver where it's probably pouring rain every day and — "

"Give me rain!" said Clarice dramatically. "I never thought I'd love Vancouver rain so much. After this fiery furnace, I'll never complain about rain, ever again."

Sadie shook off her sandals angrily and

balanced them on the window ledge to dry. Clarice had already collapsed onto her narrow bed. Accustomed to the girls' occasional spats of bickering, Brick settled himself comfortably on the rug between the two beds, stretching and yawning, and blinking lazily up at the coved ceiling with sleepy eyes. Brick had his own room on the second floor, but preferred to be with Clarice and Sadie during the day. The girls' room was on the third floor, next to Sadie's parents.

When her parents had first told Sadie they were planning a trip to Greece, she had been ecstatic. "Wow! I did Greece for my social studies project! All those ruins thousands of years old — I can't wait!"

"Good," said Mrs. Stewart, beaming at her daughter with approval. "That's not all, dear. Your father and I have a surprise for you."

"A surprise?"

"We thought it would be lovely if you invited your two friends along, isn't that right, Edgar?"

Mr. Stewart smiled happily.

Sadie stared. "Friends?"

Her mother said, "I'm sure they would benefit enormously from the exposure to so much culture — "

"You mean *Clarice?*"

" — and so much learning."

"And *Brick?*" Sadie's mouth gaped open.

"Parents can't be everything to their children," said her father, who was very modern in his thinking. "You need your friends, Sadie. Good friends are hard to come by." He smiled. "They would be company for you. Right, Esme?"

"Quite right, dear," said Mrs. Stewart.

"Thanks," said Sadie doubtfully, "That's very nice of you, but Clarice and Brick wouldn't like Greek history and myths and ancient ruins. They'd be bored right out of their braincases. They'd blame me for dragging them along, I know they would."

"Nonsense, dear," said Mrs. Stewart.

"Their parents would never let them go, anyway."

"Their parents have already agreed," said Mrs. Stewart.

"We wanted it to be a surprise," said Mr. Stewart, "so we cleared it with the O'Briens and the Chumley-Smythes first." Brick's birth name was Leopold Chumley-Smythe.

"It's all arranged," said Mrs. Stewart. "The

other parents agreed. 'A marvellous inspiration,' they said."

"They're probably just glad to be rid of them," Sadie had said, shaking her head.

Now, having worn themselves out with their bickering, the girls rested on their beds in silence. Brick began to snore.

"We should get cleaned up before dinner," murmured Sadie. But they made no move. The six o'clock dinner gong was still half an hour off.

Sadie rolled off her bed, avoiding Brick's skinny body, and stood at the open window to look out on the view. The Ariadne Hotel over-looked the Agora. Across the road from the hotel, she could see the graveyard with its broken columns and tombstones, and beyond the graveyard the high Agora fence.

She breathed in the heavy foreign smells of the air and let her thoughts wander out over the tops of the dusty-green olive trees in the hotel courtyard. The noisy clatter of cicadas reminded Sadie of the evening songs of frogs back home in Vancouver's False Creek, six thousand miles away. She shivered with pleasure. It was excit-ing to be so far from home. Greece was exactly like its travel posters: white-and-blue churches and shimmering cottages under a deep blue sky; ancient temples and ancient stories; whitewashed villages and marble statues; heroes and heroines, gods and goddesses! Sadie breathed a deep sigh of contentment.

Beyond the graveyard, inside the fenced Agora, the Temple of Vulcan stood as it had stood more than two thousand years ago, its tall columns backlit by the bright evening sun. Across from the temple was the museum. Sadie could just make out its high doors, closed for the night. In the far distance, behind the Agora, on the high hill known as the Acropolis, was the graceful Parthenon sitting atop the Acropolis like a crown.

Sadie sighed again. "I wish we could stay longer. There's so much to see. Greece is the most exciting place in the whole world!"

"Hottest place in the world, too!" said Clarice, fanning herself with her Athens street map.

"Minotaur," murmured Brick in his sleep.

Clarice said, "I'm sorry, Sadie. I didn't mean to sound ungrateful. Your folks were generous to bring me and Brick. It's the heat; it makes me feel like a fried egg."

"That's okay."

"What's the story on this monster, Sadie, the one who eats teenagers?"

Sadie, without taking her eyes from the view, said, "Nobody really knows how the gold ring comes into it."

"So why don't you tell the story while we're waiting for dinner?"

"No. I don't feel like it."

"Please, Sadie," said Clarice in her sweetest voice. "You're still mad at me for what I said about this trip."

"No, I'm not."

"You're so good at telling stories," said Clarice. She leaned down and poked Brick in the ribs. He opened one eye. "Wake up!" said Clarice. "Sadie is going to tell us the monster story."

"Sorry," said Sadie, not wanting to interrupt her mood of contentment, "I can't. Not now. Later maybe. Or borrow my book and read it for yourselves."

Brick closed his eyes again. Clarice said, "Meanie!"

The gong sounded for dinner. Clarice frowned at her watch. "They're early tonight." She jumped up off her bed. "Let's go."

Brick unfolded himself off the floor. Sadie

turned slowly from the window, reluctant to leave the view.

"Dinnertime!" said Mrs. Stewart, poking her head in the door. "Don't forget to wash, you grubby lot." Her head disappeared.

They washed their hands and then trooped down the stairs.

Although the Ariadne dining room had worn carpets and faded pink table linen, it was clean and cared for. The Agora side of the room led into a treed courtyard, which happened to be under Clarice and Sadie's room window. The tables were circular and seated four. Dinner at the Ariadne was usually a casual buffet affair. This evening it was moussaka and salad. The Lakers were already there, lined up at the buffet, helping themselves noisily. The detectives chose a table near the courtyard and sat down. Mr. and Mrs. Stewart were in conversation with the manager in the hotel lobby, so they waited.

"Mind if I join you?"

It was the good-looking Laker boy who had been staring at the gold ring as the detectives were leaving the museum. He smiled down at them. Without waiting for an answer he put his plate on the table and sat in the vacant chair.

"Help yourself," said Sadie sarcastically. She wasn't sure if she liked this boy. She had noticed him before, at Delphi, when they had been looking at the row of statues along the Sacred Way. Though very good-looking, with thick dark hair and liquid brown eyes, the boy had a smooth, superior air that put her off.

"You kids were at the museum this afternoon," said the boy with a smile, "and I saw you at Delphi. You Canadians?"

"That's right," said Sadie, noticing the patronising way he said "kids." "I bet it was the maple leaves on our diapers that gave us away."

The boy narrowed his eyes at Sadie's sarcasm. He turned to Clarice. "I'm Canadian too. Max Darcy from Ontario. I play clarinet in the Erin Lake Junior High School band."

Clarice said, "We're from Vancouver. I'm Clarice and this is Sadie and Brick."

Brick said nothing.

Sadie said, "We heard your band play at Olympia. That's been the highlight of our trip so far." Max Darcy ignored her and continued to speak to Clarice. "You look like you might be in grade eight, same as me."

"Not yet," said Clarice.

Sadie looked at her friend, trying to see her through Max Darcy's eyes. Did Clarice really look like an eighth grade girl? Or was Max merely flattering her in his smooth way? Clarice was taller this year, but she still looked like the about-to-become seventh grader she really was, Sadie decided. Still, Clarice's red hair *was* eye-catching, and with her high cheekbones and glittering green eyes, she looked interesting, like a solemn fox. If Clarice was a fox, thought Sadie ruefully, then teeth and cheeks make me a chipmunk. She sighed.

Sadie's mom and dad left the hotel manager and sat at the table next to their three charges. "Hello," said Mr. Stewart cheerfully.

"This is Max Darcy," said Sadie, "from Ontario. He plays clarinet in that high school band, the one that played in Olympia, remember?"

"You poor boy," said Mrs. Stewart sympathetically.

Back in their room, after dinner, Sadie mimicked, "You look like you might be in grade eight, same as me!" Brick lay on the rug, arms behind his head, eyes closed; Clarice sprawled lifelessly on her bed; Sadie sat at the window, squinting out at the great orange ball of the sun, now low in the sky, setting behind the Acropolis.

Clarice laughed. "That was funny."

"Funny!" said Sadie. "Didn't you hear how he was putting us down, calling us *kids* in that tone of voice? Max Darcy thinks he's so cool and mature."

"How about telling us that monster story now, Sadie?" said Clarice.

"Oh, all right," said Sadie, "but you've got to promise not to inter— "

Sadie stopped and clapped her hands to her ears as the sudden screech of a siren came from the direction of the museum.

"*Whoooeeeoo!*" the siren shrieked.

Brick sprang to his feet and glided rapidly to the window. Clarice leaped off her bed and followed him.

"What is it?" yelled Clarice.

"It's coming from the museum!" yelled Sadie. "Look!" She pointed to a backlit figure running like an Olympic athlete from the museum to the Agora fence. "It's a kid!" She shielded her eyes from the glare of the sun.

The siren screamed.

The shadowed runner leaped and climbed easily over the high wire fence, dropped lightly down into the ancient graveyard, skipped around and over marble gravestones, vaulted over a gap in the graveyard wall, dashed across the narrow street, and disappeared into the Ariadne Hotel.

 # Chapter 3

"He ran into the Ariadne!" cried Sadie.

"Let's go!" Clarice sped to the door and wrenched it open, but already it was too late: the corridor was full of alarmed hotel guests, adults and children. If the fence-jumper had managed to get to the first floor he or she would be impossible to identify in the crowd of people.

The siren wailed.

Sadie and Brick wove through the hotel guests, following Clarice along the corridor and down the stairs. Except for Mr. Pappas, the hotel manager, the lobby was empty. "Mr. Pappas," shouted Clarice above the noise of the siren, "did you see anyone run into the lobby just now?"

Mr. Pappas shook his head. "I see nobody." He smiled, trying to calm the hotel guests who were now beginning to swarm into the lobby. "Please, no prob*lem*, only museum alarm!" His hands fluttered helplessly over his ample stomach.

Clarice had to raise her voice even more to get the manager's attention again. "Were you here on the desk when that siren went off?"

"Siren? Yes. Is museum alarm," said Mr. Pappas with a strained smile. "I hear and come running from kitchen."

"And you didn't see anybody come through those doors?" Clarice persisted, pointing to the hotel entrance.

Mr. Pappas shrugged his shoulders and raised his hands, palms up. "I see nobody," he said again.

"Come on," said Clarice, heading for the door. "Let's check out the museum."

They ran along the narrow street, beside the Agora fence.

The police were already there: two cars blocked the Agora entrance. Two uniformed officers stood on guard at the fence. A small crowd had gathered. Clarice pushed her way to the front. Sadie and Brick followed. Clarice produced her

ID and waved it at the police officers. "We're Detectives," she said importantly. Clarice started to head for the museum.

The officers blocked her way, barking at her in Greek.

"If it's a Robbery, then we can help with the Investigation," Clarice explained patiently. "We're Private Detectives!" She flashed her card again.

"Is not permitted to come in," said one of the men.

"Hmmph!" said Clarice.

"Was anything stolen?" Sadie asked the policeman, hoping the answer was no, not wanting to become involved in one of Clarice's cases with so little time left of the holiday.

"Is not permitted," said the policeman.

"Let's go," said Clarice. "We're wasting time. We won't get anything out of them."

They hurried back along the wire fence toward the hotel.

"I have a Hunch," said Clarice.

Sadie sighed. "You and your so-called hunches, Clarice — "

Clarice looked grim. "My Hunch, Number Two, is that someone stole that gold ring."

Sadie noticed with dismay that her friend was not only starting to salt her statements with capital letters but was also calling her by her detective name. Which meant that Clarice had definitely switched to case-solving mode. The holiday was deteriorating fast.

"I think so, too, Chief," said Brick who was balancing himself like a tightrope artist on the top of the Agora fence.

Sadie simply sighed.

When they got back to the hotel, they found the manager behind the reception desk with his companion, a sleek black cat named Aphrodite who spent most of her day sleeping on the blotter. "Mr. Pappas," said Clarice, "did you hear yet what happened at the museum?"

Mr. Angelo Pappas was a kindly, helpful man who did his best to make his guests happy. He was very proud that he spoke such excellent English. He jerked his plump chin at the radio. "A most bold robbing, dear child. The bold robber robbed sacred ring of the House of Athens!"

Clarice and Sadie gave each other meaningful looks.

"Is priceless, this ring," continued Mr. Pappas, "a part of Greek history; it cannot be replaced." He threw up his hands. "Is like thief stealing death mask of Agamemnon, or painting of Mona Lisa. Is only one in whole world."

"The ring is made of gold, isn't it, Mr. Pappas?" said Clarice.

"Ah, yes, gold is worth much money, but is not the gold." Mr. Pappas' hands fluttered over his plump stomach like birds. "Is the sacred history, you understand?"

Clarice nodded. "Do the police know who took the ring?"

Mr. Pappas shook his head. "Police soon catch bold bad robber."

Clarice said, "Mr. Pappas, are there any other kids staying at the hotel — besides us and the Erin Lake school band, I mean?"

"Kids?" Mr. Pappas chewed on this new word. "No," he said at last, "no other kids."

"Thanks, Mr. Pappas," said Clarice.

"No prob*lem*." Mr. Pappas smiled broadly.

"Well, we've got ourselves a Case," said Clarice excitedly when they were upstairs in their room. "It *was* the gold ring. My Hunch was right! You want to know my second Hunch?"

Sadie sighed. She had known somehow, way back when her parents had planned the trip, that her happy contemplation of Greek culture would be interrupted by Clarice's thirst for business. At least it had come near the end of the trip. Things could be worse. She tried to smile. "What *is* your second hunch, Clarice?"

"My second Hunch is that a Laker kid stole the ring."

"That's no hunch," said Sadie, slipping out of her still damp sandals and propping them up on the window ledge again to dry. "It's a clever deduction. Look at the facts: first, we see a bunch of kids eyeballing the gold ring like they'd kill for it; second, we see a kid jump over the Agora fence as the alarm goes off; third, the kid runs into our hotel; fourth, the only other kids here are the Lakers. Therefore, one of the Lakers stole the ring." Sadie shrugged. "That's no hunch, it's just smart thinking."

"Thanks, Number Two," said Clarice at Sadie's unintended compliment.

Brick had settled himself on the rug, but this time, instead of napping, he seemed to be listening carefully to everything the girls had to say.

Clarice kicked off her sandals. "Do you remember which Laker kids were staring into the gold ring case as we were getting thrown out of the museum?"

Sadie winced at the reminder. "There were four of them: the smart-aleck kid named Kerry; Max Smooth-talk Darcy; and two girls."

"That right, Number Three?"

"That's right, Chief."

"Then they're our Primary Suspects," said Clarice.

"Wait a minute," said Sadie. "It couldn't be Max Darcy. He ate dinner with us."

"Unless he went back to the museum right after dinner," said Clarice.

"Not enough time," said Sadie. "Whoever we saw jumping over the fence had to have been in the museum during dinner."

"I agree," said Clarice. "Which leaves only three primary suspects: Kerry and the two girls."

"Did the fence-climber look like a girl to you?" said Sadie.

"Hard to say," said Clarice. "The sun was too bright behind him. Or her. All we can be sure of is that it was a kid."

"I'm worried," said Sadie.

"About what?"

"If the police discover it's one of the kids at

this hotel, then we'll *all* share the shame and disgrace! Our country will be dishonoured! Trashed! The name of Canada will be mud for ever!"

 **Chapter 4**

Clarice threw herself onto her bed and raked her fingers through her hair. "You're right, Number Two. The Honour of Canada is at stake!"

Sadie sat thoughtfully on the window chair; Brick was still sitting cross-legged and wide awake on the rug.

"Maybe we can find the ring and smuggle it back somehow," said Sadie. "Then nobody need ever know how close Canada came to international disgrace. I think we should go talk to the primary suspects right now, and demand the ring be handed over."

"Not so fast," said Clarice. "We need to talk it over, examine the possibilities."

"Brainstorm," said Brick, nodding.

"We need to know the Motive," said Clarice. "If we discover the Motive, then we're on our way to discovering the Thief."

"The motive is pretty obvious," said Sadie. "That ring is no ordinary ring: it's got supernatural properties. Whoever wears it would be like the hero, Prince Theseus, or like Mario Lemieux or Shaquille O'Neal. He'd have incredible strength and speed."

"Like Superman," said Brick.

"Well, not quite," said Sadie. "I don't expect he'd be able to fly, lift a Greyhound bus, leap over tall buildings in a single bound or anything like that. But he'd be mega fast and strong."

"As far as I'm concerned," said Clarice, "it's just an ugly old ring. But it's a gold one."

"Well, I believe it's got powers," said Sadie. "And whoever stole it believes it too. There's your motive, Clarice."

"You could be right, Number Two," said Clarice, "but I'm not sure that's enough of a motive for such a serious crime. I can't believe a kid would commit a crime because he wants to be a great hockey player."

"Or basketball player, or marathon runner," said Sadie.

"Or even a great dancer?" said Clarice.

"Of course," said Sadie.

"Hmmmm," said Clarice. "Let's say you're right about the motive, where does that get us? Everyone wants to be a hero. It could be anybody!"

"Not anybody," said Sadie. "Unless there's someone who can be in two places at the same time, then it isn't anyone who was at dinner."

Clarice rolled off her bed. "Let's go ask the Laker teacher, Miss Plum, if any of them missed dinner. She should know."

"They're in the courtyard," said Sadie. Her slightly prominent ears were very powerful, even concealed as they usually were by her long hair, and she had already picked up the sound of the two teachers murmuring together below the window. "Oh, Allan," murmured Miss Plum. "Ah, Daphne," murmured Mr. Pollon.

The three sleuths trooped down the stairs. "Don't tell them what we suspect," said Clarice. "No sense in stressing them out."

Miss Plum and Mr. Pollon were seated at a small table under an olive tree, with long, cool drinks.

"Excuse me," said Clarice, "but can you tell

us if any of your band people missed dinner tonight?"

The two teachers looked at Clarice in surprise.

Sadie stepped forward. "We're from Vancouver, British Columbia. I'm Sadie Stewart, and this is Clarice O'Brien."

Brick coughed quietly.

"And this is Brick," said Clarice. "We heard your band play at Olympia."

"We'll never forget it," said Sadie.

Miss Plum smiled. "Thank you. As a matter of fact, Sadie, several band members missed dinner. Why do you ask?"

Clarice said, "We just wondered if maybe, uh . . . "

"If anyone was too tired or sick after all that heat today," put in Sadie quickly. "Lost their appetite, you know?"

"It's funny you should ask," said Miss Plum, "because so many of them missed dinner this evening."

"Four," said Mr. Pollon. "Most unusual."

"Who were they?" said Clarice.

Miss Plum thought for a second, and then said, "There was Ann, Ann Furey that is. Kerry

Krohn, Jennifer Hill . . . and the girl who chews gum all the time — "

"Gloria Platt," said Mr. Pollon.

"They were sick?" said Clarice.

"I don't think so," said Miss Plum. "Mr. Pollon and I checked with them after dinner. They said they weren't hungry. It *was* a particularly hot day yesterday."

"Well, thanks," said Clarice.

Mr. Pollon narrowed his eyes suspiciously. "Are you sure there's nothing wrong?"

"You're right, it was probably the heat," said Sadie. "We just wondered, that's all."

As they passed by the hotel desk, Mr. Pappas' cat said, "Prrrmmnng."

Brick answered, "Hrrrmmnnghh," and Aphrodite jumped down off the counter and followed him upstairs.

In the girls' room they took their usual places, Sadie near the window, Brick on the rug with Aphrodite curled up, purring, on his skinny chest, and Clarice cross-legged on her bed. Sadie had her notebook out and was writing in it with such concentration that the tip of her tongue could be seen peeping out from between her teeth. "We've made those two teachers suspicious," said Clarice. "Better write those four names down before we forget them, Number Two."

Sadie sighed a know-it-all sigh. "I already did, Clarice."

"We're on a Case now. You can start calling me Chief."

"Yes, Clarice."

Clarice said, "We must remember our three Primary Suspects: the first is the girl who dances, the second is the girl with the dark curly hair, and the third is Kerry Krohn. They were the ones gathered around the gold ring case with Max Darcy. Kerry missed dinner, we know that much already. So did three others. Why? They told Miss Plum they weren't hungry. But one of them might be lying. One of them might have missed dinner because he or she was busy stealing the gold ring from the museum."

Brick said, "Good work, Chief."

Aphrodite purred louder.

"Good work, Chief!" Sadie mimicked sarcastically. She pulled off her glasses and started polishing the lenses furiously.

Clarice rubbed absently at the lighter patches left by sandal straps on her bare foot.

"So so far we have three Primary Suspects, and four people who missed dinner. What were the names Miss Plum mentioned, Number Two?"

Without looking in her notebook, Sadie said, "Gloria Platt, Jennifer Hill, Ann Furey. Here, take a look." She tossed the notebook over to Clarice.

Sadie had written:

Kids seen in museum eyeballing ring — primary suspects

1. girl dancer

2. girl with dark curly hair

3. Kerry Krohn

Kids who missed dinner

1. Jennifer Hill

2. Ann Furey

3. Gloria Platt (gum chewer)

4. Kerry Krohn

"Well done, Number Two!"

"Thanks, Clarice."

Clarice passed the notebook to Brick. "We can spot them at breakfast," said Clarice. "I'll ask Max Darcy to help us identify them."

Silence, except for Aphrodite's purr.

"How do you suppose the robber pulled it off?" said Sadie.

Clarice said, "Probably hid in the museum at closing time. Then when the guards had gone, he or she stole the ring from the case and broke out of the museum, which set off the alarm. Then he made a run for the fence."

"Right," said Sadie. "Probably hid in the washroom."

"Or in that big water jar," said Clarice.

"Good idea, Chief," said Brick.

"Tomorrow," said Clarice, "we question the suspects."

Brick yawned and stretched. Aphrodite stepped daintily off his chest onto the rug. Brick rolled up off the floor and was gone out the door, Aphrodite padding along behind him, before the girls had even a chance to bid him goodnight.

# Chapter 5

Breakfast in the Ariadne courtyard was always the same — orange juice, corn flakes with goat's milk, hard-boiled eggs, rolls and butter and preserves — but there was plenty of it.

It was only eight o'clock and already it was hot. Several hotel cats sprawled under the shade trees.

Sadie and Clarice were busy eating. Brick sipped at his juice quietly and closed his eyes. His yellow eyelashes were very long. The girls seldom knew what Brick thought about. He seemed to be enjoying the sun on his face. Mr. Pappas' cat lay curled up in his lap.

Clarice reached for another boiled egg. "I've

decided I'm tired of foreign food. I've also decided to stay close to Granville Island for the rest of my life and travel no more."

"Remind me to tell my mom and dad how much you're enjoying this trip."

"Sorry, Number Two. I didn't mean I'm not actually enjoying myself. If I could only have some Canadian pancakes now and then, with Canadian maple syrup, I'd be fine."

"If you're still planning to be a world-famous detective," said Sadie, "then you'll have to travel."

"No I won't. Sherlock Holmes never left England. I plan to live in a houseboat in Sea Village on Granville Island, Vancouver, British Columbia, and when anyone wants a crime solved they will have to travel to me."

Sadie sighed. Brick grinned.

"We've got lots to do today," said Clarice. "We've got to Interview the Suspects and ask Searching Questions, and there's also the Scene of the Crime to check out."

Sadie pushed away her plate, and stretched like a cat in the yellow warmth. She thought of how Clarice changed, became livelier, whenever she had a case to solve: her eyes flashed, her speech became vigorous, she spoke in earnest capitals. Her authority was so total that even eighth graders listened to her with awe and respect. At times like these Sadie was proud to be her friend. The only place she drew a line was at the word "Chief." She just could not bring herself to use that word.

"Let's find out where the Lakers are going today," said Clarice, now stuffing herself with a roll and strawberry jam, "and go with them. That will give us an opportunity to question the suspects."

"I see Max Darcy," said Sadie. "He's with the dark-haired girl, one of the suspects." She nodded her head in the direction of Max's table.

"Come on," said Clarice, brushing the crumbs off the front of her T-shirt and lurching up from the table.

Sadie and Brick followed.

"Hi," said Clarice. "Can we join you two for a minute?"

Max Darcy smiled and pulled out a chair for Clarice to sit. The dark-haired girl got up quickly and left.

"Who was that?" said Clarice.

"Ann Furey," said Max.

So, one of the primary suspects was Ann Furey, thought Sadie. She had been one of the foursome staring greedily at the ring, and, more importantly, had missed dinner.

"What's the name of that girl over there, the one who said yesterday she wants to be a famous dancer?" Clarice pointed to the tall, willowy girl who was sitting several tables away near the two teachers.

"That's Jennifer Hill."

Sadie pulled out her notebook and began scribbling furiously.

"And the one sitting over there with Kerry?" Clarice continued.

"You know Kerry?" said Max, surprised.

"Not really," said Clarice, "but we talked with him yesterday."

"Kerry's with Gloria Platt." Max smiled easily. "Why do you want to know their names?"

"They all missed dinner yesterday," said Clarice.

Max shrugged. "So?"

Clarice took a deep breath and, keeping her voice low so that Miss Plum and Mr. Pollon at the next table would not overhear, said, "We believe someone from your group stole the gold

NAME	In Museum?	Missed dinner?	Primary Suspect
Jennifer Hill (dancer)	Yes	Yes	Yes
Ann Furey (dark curly hair)	Yes	Yes	Yes
Kerry Krohn (smart aleck)	Yes	Yes	Yes
Max Darcy (smoothy)	Yes	No	No
Gloria Platt (gum chewer)	No	Yes	Maybe

ring from the museum yesterday while we were all having dinner."

Max stared at her. So did Sadie. Clarice didn't usually share her investigations with outsiders. Sadie hoped Clarice hadn't succumbed to Max's oily charm.

"We saw a kid jump the fence and run into the Ariadne," whispered Clarice. "The only kids in the hotel are your bunch."

Max chuckled. "No way. A kid couldn't pull off a serious crime like that. And even if he could, I'm sure it isn't a member of the band." He raised his eyebrows at the three sleuths. "But what's it to you, anyway?"

"We're Detectives," said Clarice. "We solve Crimes."

Max smiled. "Kid detectives! That's great. Like Nancy Drew. Be careful you don't get into trouble." He chuckled again, and winked at Clarice. Sadie suppressed an impulse to gag.

Clarice stood. "Where are you all going today?" she said in her normal voice. "Maybe we'll be bumping into you again."

"Morning shopping in the Plaka," said Max.

The Plaka, a popular tourist area of Athens, was the old town at the foot of the Acropolis. It consisted of a maze of narrow streets crowded with shops. Clarice, Brick and the Stewarts had already been there. All the shopkeepers closed between two and six each day for a siesta, but then opened again until after midnight.

"And then it's the War Museum in the afternoon," said Max, "followed by a bus trip to Poseidon's Temple."

"Maybe we'll see you in the War Museum," said Clarice.

"Happy detecting," said Max.

Mr. Pollon turned his head. "You and your parents are welcome to share our bus to the War Museum if you like," he said to Clarice. "We leave right after lunch."

"Thanks," said Clarice and Sadie together.

Clarice led the way over to the table where Kerry and Gloria were sitting, talking and laughing, black paintbrush and sun-bleached pageboy close together.

"Could we ask you two a few questions?" said Clarice.

"No, we're busy," said Kerry.

Gloria was chewing gum. She blew a bubble. "What do you want to ask us about?"

"We're Canadians," said Clarice. "Like you.

We think Canadians should stick together and help each other."

"Are you a politician or what?" said Kerry in his smart-alecky voice.

"No," said Clarice. "We're detectives. A valuable gold ring was stolen from the museum. We think one of your group stole it. We want to get it back so our country is not disgraced."

"You should run for Prime Minister," said Kerry. "You'd be better at that than being a detective."

"We don't give interviews to kid detectives," said Gloria with a sneer.

Sadie stepped forward. "This is important. We need to know where you were — "

"Get lost, kids," said Gloria.

"Beat it!" said Kerry.

Brick pushed himself forward. His amber eyes glowed.

"Come on," said Clarice to Brick, taking him by the arm, "there's no sense in losing our tempers." She led the way toward Sadie's parents' table.

"Mrs. Stewart," said Clarice, "do you mind if we spend the morning in the Agora and the museum again?"

Mrs. Stewart was pleased. "It *is* good to see the three of you becoming so interested in ancient Greek history and archaeology."

"We're *very* interested," admitted Clarice.

Mrs. Stewart said, "We'll be ready in twenty minutes. Be sure to bring your hats and carry plenty of water."

"*Nero*," said Brick. Sadie knew from her phrasebook that it meant water. Brick seemed to be picking up a lot of Greek words and phrases.

"And could we go to the War Museum this afternoon?" said Sadie. "Mr. Pollon, the band teacher, said we can all go with them on their bus."

Her parents beamed with delight. "We would love to go," said Mrs. Stewart.

Clarice said, "After the War Museum, they're going on a bus trip to — what is it, Sadie?"

"Poseidon's Temple."

"That's it," said Clarice. "Could we all go too, do you think?"

Mrs. Stewart frowned. "I'm not sure where — "

"It's at Cape Sounion," said Sadie. "A short bus ride along the coast road. You wouldn't want to miss it, Mom. It's a must-see."

❋   ❋   ❋

They lined up for tickets at the Agora entrance. Once inside the fence, they separated, Mr. and Mrs. Stewart to wander around the Temple of Vulcan, and the three friends to examine the crime scene.

Inside the museum it seemed to be business as usual. But the Theseus cabinet had been removed entirely, and a different one, full of pottery shards and small jars, had been put in its place. There was nothing to show that a serious crime had been committed the day before.

The detectives trod softly around the new cabinet searching for clues.

Clarice bent down and picked up a tiny sliver of glass from under the new case. She showed it to Sadie. "Looks like the glass of the Theseus case was smashed."

"Smash-and-grab," agreed Sadie.

"Ti — kanetê esê ta pidia?"

It was a security guard, a large, dark man with a mustache like a shoe brush.

"Good morning, officer," said Sadie with a disarming smile. The guard scowled.

"Let's move on," muttered Clarice. The guard watched them suspiciously as they wandered off along the gallery.

When the guard was out of sight, they inspected the amphora that Sadie had been trapped in the day before, looking for tell-tale marks. It was Sadie who noticed scrapes and scuff marks on the shoulder of the jar. "I know those marks weren't there when I got out yesterday. Besides, I didn't climb onto the shoulder, Brick heaved me up and I rolled in. These marks could have been caused by the thief."

"You're right, Number Two," said Clarice. "They weren't there yesterday. And climbing out is tough. Must be someone tall and strong in the arms."

While they had been talking, Brick had found the possible point of break-out: several high windows opened outward above exhibit cases along the wall. He pointed at one of them without saying anything. It was open. Then he pointed to the cabinet underneath. "Looks like the thief climbed up onto this cabinet," said Clarice, "pushed the window open, and climbed out."

"With the gold ring," said Sadie, nodding.

Clarice peered closely at the scratches and scuff marks on the top of the cabinet. "Some of these scratches look new — probably from the thief's shoes."

When they got outside, the sun was hot. Clarice pointed. "Next, we walk a straight route from the open window to the fence where we saw the thief climb over. Spread out a bit, and eyeball every inch of the ground for clues."

It was much too hot to hurry. They took their time walking across the wide Agora, past the toppled remains of Corinthian columns and ancient altars, past the Temple of Vulcan, to the high fence. They found nothing. They could see the graveyard and the entrance of their hotel through the wire mesh.

"Let's get out of the sun," said Clarice. "I'm thirsty."

The three detectives sat down upon an ancient remnant of broken column under the shade of a laurel tree. They drank from their water bottles. Clarice and Sadie took off their hats and fanned themselves. Brick wore no hat; the heat didn't seem to affect him.

"So far, so good," said Clarice. "I think we have a good picture of the crime. This is the way it looks: the Perp hid for — "

"The what?" said Sadie.

"The Perp," said Clarice. "Short for Perpetrator. The police hardly ever say criminal or thief any more. It's Perp. Anyway, the Perp hid for almost an hour in the amphora waiting until the guards had gone and the cleaning staff had finished. When the museum was empty he, or she, climbed out of the jar, smashed the case, and grabbed the ring."

"I think that jerk Kerry Krohn is the Perp," said Sadie. "He probably smashed the case with one of those small marble statues, the ones on the shelves."

Clarice nodded. "Then he — or she — climbed up on top of the exhibit case, released the lock and pushed the window open. The alarm went off. He climbed through the window, dropped to the ground, and ran for the fence. Which is when we saw him. Have I got it right so far?"

Sadie and Brick nodded their agreement.

Clarice continued, "Motive is next. Maybe it's the gold, maybe it's that guff about supernatural power, but whoever stole the ring was greedy for something. So we know *How* the Crime was committed, we know *When*, and we have a theory *Why*. All we don't know for sure is *Who*."

Brick stared at Clarice. "Wow!" he whispered. Sadie got up off the marble column and lay down under the shade of the tree. She gazed up through the laurel branches at the vast blueness of the Greek sky.

"The Lakers should all be back before lunch, so we can talk to some of the suspects then," said Clarice. "We have to act fast and get the ring back before the police start asking awkward questions."

Sadie glanced at her watch. "That's still an hour away."

"Then tell us the story of Theseus and the Minotaur," said Clarice, joining Sadie on the grass. "Why did the monster eat only teenagers?"

"Because teenagers are the best age for flavour and tenderness, of course," said Sadie. "If I tell the story, you've got to promise not to interrupt. I can't stand it when I'm telling someone something and they keep interrupting."

"Brick and I won't say a word, right, Number Three?"

"Right, Chief."

"You didn't promise."

"We promise," said Clarice. "Not one word."

 **Chapter 6**

Brick swung himself up easily into the laurel tree over Sadie's head, and was greeted by a chorus of chirping cicadas. He lay back along a thick limb and closed his eyes.

Sadie looked around her at the broken columns, the temple, and, in the distance, white cottages crowded together on a hillside beyond the Agora. She felt good. A slight breeze carried with it the exotic Mediterranean smells of ripening olives, lotus, myrtle and acanthus. She gazed up into the foliage of the cool tree and the blue sky beyond. She could see Brick's ragged sneakers above her. She thought for a minute, and then began her story.

"The Minotaur was imprisoned in the Labyrinth."

"In the what?" said Clarice.

"Labyrinth," said Brick, who was listening very attentively.

Clarice rolled onto her side and looked up at Brick in the tree. "What's a Labyrinth?"

"I dunno." He opened one eye and peered down at Sadie.

"It was a maze of passages that twisted and turned and ran around and doubled back into themselves, and because it was deep underneath King Minos' palace no sunlight ever penetrated its darkness. King Minos of Crete imprisoned the Minotaur there, and each year he fed the Minotaur fourteen teenagers from conquered Athens."

Clarice pulled a stalk of grass and began chewing it thoughtfully.

"The Athens teenagers became the regular menu," continued Sadie. "They wandered helplessly around the dark Labyrinth and the Minotaur devoured them. One at a time."

"Horrible!" said Clarice. "This story is putting me off my lunch."

"Actually," said Sadie, "nobody knows if the

Minotaur ate one teenager a month, saving the extra couple for special feast days, or if he ate the whole fourteen and then slept until the next year. Nobody ever escaped to tell the tale, and the underground passageways became littered with the bones of teenagers."

"So tell about how Theseus killed the monster," said Clarice.

"When Theseus reached the age of sixteen," said Sadie, "he asked his father if he could go to King Minos' palace across the sea to kill the Minotaur.

" 'I will join this year's group of fourteen,' said the young prince.

"King Aegeus was horrified. 'Theseus! You're out of your adolescent mind! Are you losing brain cells or what? You're my only son. You'll be king of Athens one day. You can't go. That's final!' "

"Typical parent reaction," said Clarice. "A kid wants to go off and have an adventure, maybe get himself killed, and all a parent can say is — "

"Clarice!"

"Sorry."

"What with your interruptions, Clarice, and the noise from this tree, I can't hear myself speak."

Clarice leaned back on her elbows and looked up into the dark green foliage of the tree. "What are those screechy things anyway?"

"Cicadas," said Sadie.

"Sick what?" said Clarice.

"Insects," said Sadie. "Like big grasshoppers."

"Why can't I see them?"

"Camouflage," said Sadie loudly.

"Why do they make such a racket?"

"They're mating," said Sadie. She was almost shouting. "The males are the ones who make all the noise." The cicadas were becoming noisier. Sadie clutched her throat. "I think I'm losing my voice."

Brick yelled, "Kkklllkk gang-gang."

The cicadas stopped their clicking. The metallic hum disappeared. The tree was silent. It was as though a switch had been turned off.

Brick seemed to have a way with animals.

"Thanks," said Sadie. She drank from her water bottle, then continued telling the story. " 'How can you send other young people of Athens and favour your own son?' said Theseus. 'If I don't go, we're both unworthy to rule.'

" 'I'm the king, and the word of the king is

final. Besides, this monster cannot be killed with knives or swords or any weapon made by man, because his real father was a god.'

" 'You don't say! Then I'll use my bare hands,' said Theseus.

" 'You can't go!'

" 'The honour of the House of Athens is more important than the death of a prince,' said Theseus. 'I'm sorry, Father, but I must go.'

"So he went. He sailed with thirteen other teens to Crete. And when King Minos' daughter, whose name was Ariadne, saw Theseus stepping ashore and saw how hunky he was, she fell in love with him at first sight."

"But that's the same name as our hotel!" said Clarice. "The Ariadne Hotel!"

"That's right, Clarice. It's named after her. Ariadne couldn't possibly allow Theseus to die in the Labyrinth, so she came to him in the cell where he and his friends were being kept for the night and she said, 'I love you with all my heart. My name is Ariadne, and my father is King Minos. He would be very angry if he knew I were here.'

" 'My name is Theseus, and my father is the King of Athens.'

" 'I've come to help you,' said Ariadne. 'I can't let you die.'

" 'You are very beautiful,' said Theseus."

Clarice said, "Did they kiss?"

Sadie ignored the interruption. "Ariadne gave Theseus a lantern, and a ball of twine to unwind as he and his friends penetrated the Labyrinth. 'When my father's guards leave you in the middle of the Labyrinth, the twine and the lantern will lead you back to my waiting arms,' she told him.

"So that's what Theseus did. He didn't let the guards see Ariadne's lantern, nor did they notice the twine being unwound behind them as they walked through the echoing black passageways, deeper and deeper into the Labyrinth, stumbling over the bones of teenagers from Athens who had died before them.

"After a while the fourteen kids were left by the guards, and now they were alone without light. Theseus sat down on the cold ground. The others, seven girls and six boys, begged Theseus to lead them out of the Labyrinth by following the trail of twine, but Theseus refused to move.

" 'Rest,' he told them. 'We'll let the monster find us. That way I'll be fresh for the battle.'

" 'Battle! Are you crazy? We gotta get out of here,' said the others, 'or we're Teenburgers!'

"But Theseus ordered them to stay with him in the darkness. 'I must slay this monster,' he said, 'for while it remains alive there is no freedom for the people of Athens.'

"The others sat, and they waited all that day, listening for the monster. They were totally petrified with fear.

"Theseus stretched out on the floor and closed his eyes.

"There was no sun to judge the time, but it must have been many hours later when they heard it. It started as something faint and far away, a shuffling and a moaning, and as the sounds grew louder, a snorting and a bellowing.

"Theseus didn't stir.

"The other kids started to panic. 'The monster's coming!' they cried.

"Theseus didn't move.

"The noises grew louder and louder. The monster bellowed with hunger. It was searching for them in the darkness, sniffing the air, smelling them out.

"Theseus leaped to his feet, and told his

friends to stand back out of the way. 'Light the lantern and hold it high.'

"They saw in the light from the lantern a giant of a man with hairy arms and thighs, and the head and horns of a mighty bull. He was so enormous he filled the passageway. He bellowed and roared, his eyes red with rage and hunger at the sight of the cowering teenagers."

"Half human, half animal," murmured Brick.

"Bare-handed and weaponless, the brave Theseus stepped forward and looked up at that great bull head swaying above him. 'Prepare to meet thy maker, monster of the Labyrinth,' he shouted.

"The Minotaur's roar thundered and echoed through the tunnelled passageways. 'Puny Athenian! Who art thou? And what harm canst thou with thy bare hands do a creature like me? Answer before I destroy thee!'"

"Hold it right there, Number Two," said Clarice. "How can this monster talk? He's got the head of a bull, remember?"

"Half human," said Brick.

"The head of a bull, but the neck and body of a man," replied Sadie. "He had vocal chords in his neck same as everybody. He had the sounds of a bull *and* a man."

"What happened next?" said Brick.

Sadie took a deep breath. " 'Who art thou?'
said the Minotaur."

"You already told that bit," said Clarice.

" 'I am the one destined to slay you, ugly
monster,' said Theseus, deliberately provoking
the Minotaur to anger. He knew his only chance
of success lay in outwitting this powerful giant.

" 'Thou callest me ugly monster! But what
canst thou know of me?' The Minotaur let out a
thunderous cry of agony. 'I cannot be killed by
any weapon made by man! I am doomed to pace
this dark and lonely prison in dire torment all
the days of my life! Say who thou art before I
devour thee!'

"Theseus' companions fell back in terror.

" 'My name is Theseus, only son of King
Aegeus of the Royal House of Athens.'

" 'A prince!' bellowed the monster. 'I have
never in my life eaten a prince! Aah! These horns
ache to gore royal flesh; this mouth thirsts to
taste royal blood; these jaws hunger to crush
royal bone!'

" 'And these bare hands itch to destroy the
ugly monster who has feasted on so many of

Athens' teenagers,' said Theseus bravely.

"These words had hardly left Theseus' lips when the monster, bellowing with rage, lowered his head and charged at the young prince with incredible speed. The thirteen young captives trembled with fear. The girls screamed in terror."

Clarice gave a snort of disgust. "Why is it always the girls who scream in terror? Makes me want to puke! Boys can scream too, you know! Anyway, if I had a big monster charging at me, I wouldn't have time to scream in terror, I'd be too busy jumping out of its way!"

"That's exactly what Theseus did," said Sadie. "He leaped nimbly aside and let the charging beast go by. But the tip of one of the Minotaur's horns gouged some flesh from Theseus' side, and it bled. 'How clumsy you are, Monster,' goaded Theseus, hiding his wound.

"The Minotaur became even more angry. He turned quickly and rushed again, but this time Theseus was ready: he sidestepped at the very last moment, careful to avoid those sharp horns that came tossing at him, threatening to rip out his heart. 'Why, you missed me again, Monster!' laughed Theseus. 'Have these dark passages made you blind as well as clumsy? How will you drink my blood and crush my bones if you cannot catch me?'

"Goaded by Theseus, the Minotaur got angrier and angrier, and charged many times with incredible speed and strength, but each time Theseus danced aside at the last possible moment, mocking him.

"Theseus' companions, scared half to death by the charging and the awful bellowing, pressed themselves back against the cold, damp walls that shuddered and trembled with the force of the beast's fury.

"After an hour of combat the monster was breathing hard. Theseus' side was getting a bit stiff where he'd been wounded, but he was keeping his cool. The monster's roars were not quite so loud as he charged again. He was tiring: the charge was slower and the horns did not toss so wildly. Theseus waited, balancing lightly on his toes. The monster charged, and veered to the side thinking to trick his quick-footed opponent and catch him with a deadly horn, but this time Theseus didn't sidestep; instead, he dived down between the monster's hairy legs in a rolling somersault, bounced up, and leaped up onto the Minotaur's back before he had time to turn.

"The Minotaur roared with rage. Theseus wrapped his arms around the creature's neck from behind in a stranglehold — it was the neck of a man, remember — and squeezed with all his strength, cutting off the Minotaur's air.

"The monster twisted and turned and bucked and jumped, but couldn't shake Theseus off. It wasn't long before the monster's legs weakened for lack of air. Then he collapsed. Theseus had him down, but did not slacken the grip of his muscular arms around the monster's neck. The bull eyes rolled; the tongue lolled out. The monster grew weaker and weaker. The sweat ran down Theseus' face; his biceps were about to burst, but he hung on and squeezed with all the strength he had left.

"The bull head went limp. The monster fumbled and pulled a gold ring from his finger. He tried to speak, but Theseus' hold was too tight. Theseus suspected a trick, but loosened his grip just enough so the monster could suck in a little air. 'Thou art more wily than Odysseus,' gasped the Minotaur. 'Thou hast beaten me in fair combat. Take this ring. The crippled god, Hephaestus, forged it in the fires of Mount Olympus. It is thine.'

" 'Why should I take your ring?' panted Theseus, still suspecting a trick.

"There came a rattle in the Minotaur's heaving chest. He was sinking quickly. Soon he would be dead. 'Whoever wears the ring,' he whispered faintly, 'will be strong and swift, gifts the wily Prince Theseus already has and needs not, but there is one other gift which will make him great.'

" 'What gift, Monster?'

" 'Compassion.'

"Theseus took the ring and slipped it onto his thumb, for it was too big for his finger.

" 'Poor monster,' said Theseus.

"The Minotaur managed to gasp out one choked word, then he died."

"Theseus killed him?" said Brick.

"That's right," said Sadie.

"What does compassion mean, Sadie?" said Clarice.

"It means having a tender heart," said Sadie, "and pity for the suffering of others."

"You didn't tell us what the last word was," said Clarice, "the last word of the dying Minotaur."

"The last word?" said Sadie. "It was 'Efcharistó.'"

"It was what?" said Clarice.

Brick said, "*Efcharistó* — thank you."

"That makes no sense!" Clarice objected. "Why would the monster thank him? Sadie, are you sure you told the story just the way it is in the book?"

"Great story, Number Two," said Brick.

"Thanks." Sadie glanced at her watch, and got up off the grass. "By the time we get back and question one of the suspects it'll be lunchtime."

"Kkkllkk gung-gung," said Brick. The noise of the cicadas started up again. The tree hummed. Brick climbed high into the leafy branches to meet his insect friends face-to-face.

The metallic hum of the cicadas rose to a frenzy.

"Let's move out!" yelled Clarice.

Brick dropped to the ground, grinning. "Lunch," he said happily.

 # Chapter 7

"Have they found the robber who stole the gold ring yet, Mr. Pappas?" said Sadie.

The manager sat at the hotel desk reading his newspaper. Aphrodite stretched her long neck out for Brick to rub. Mr. Pappas showed the three sleuths the news story. There was a picture of the ring on the front page.

"What does it say?" said Sadie.

"Police expect to makc arrest very soon," said Mr. Pappas. He smiled proudly. "Is no prob*lem*."

They found the willowy and perspiring Jennifer Hill playing a game of ping-pong, and were able to entice her away with the offer of a bottle of Coke in the courtyard.

Clarice introduced herself and her friends. "We'd like to ask you a few questions, Jennifer, if you don't mind," said Clarice. The foursome sat at a table in the shade with their Cokes. Aphrodite leaped up onto the table. "Puuurrrrr," she said to Brick.

"Hrrmmnngg," Brick said to Aphrodite.

"Prrmmnngg," said Aphrodite to Brick.

"Brick, would you ask your cat friend to get off the table," said Clarice.

"Hrrggofff," said Brick to Aphrodite.

The cat jumped down to the ground and lay down beside Brick's sneakers. Several other cats strolled over and lay down under the table.

Jennifer laughed. "That's quite a trick, Brick. Can you talk to all animals, or is it just cats?"

Brick didn't answer. Sadie said, "Brick talks to all animals. According to him, it's got something to do with the way he was born in Africa. He crawled out of his mosquito net, got lost in the jungle, and was brought up by lions."

"You're kidding," said Jennifer.

"But if you want my opinion," said Sadie, "his parents deliberately left him to the lions. They took one look at him when he was born and ran away from home."

Jennifer's high-pitched giggle frightened some of the cats; they ran into the hotel. "So what's this all about?" she asked, resting her pointed chin in a graceful hand.

"We think someone from your group stole that ring from the museum yesterday," said Clarice.

Jennifer's brown eyes registered no surprise.

"And we think you might be able to help us find the Perp — uh, the thief," said Clarice.

Jennifer smiled a haughty smile. "What little busybodies you are. What has the stolen ring got to do with you?"

"We're not busybodies," said Clarice, "we're Detectives. We solve Crimes."

Jennifer laughed. "Like who stole the bubblegum? Is that the kind of crime you mean?"

"What instrument do you play in the band?" said Sadie sweetly.

"Trumpet. Why?"

"Sounds to me like you blew all your brains away."

Jennifer glared at Sadie. Clarice said quickly, "Do you believe the ring has a special power, like Miss Plum said?"

"If you wear it, you're a supergirl, you mean?

I don't know." Jennifer shrugged her narrow shoulders.

"You could become the most famous dancer in the world," said Clarice.

"You think I stole the ring?" said Jennifer. "Hey, I'd love to have a ring like that, be a supergirl and all, but there's no way I would *steal* it."

"We're not saying you did," said Clarice. "Could I see your sandals?"

"Huh?"

"Would you mind slipping off your sandals so we can take a look at them?"

Jennifer bent down, unstrapped her thin sandals and handed them to Clarice, who inspected them carefully, turning them over and over, running her fingers lightly along the sole and the brown leather surfaces.

"Thanks." She handed them back. "This your only pair?"

"I've got a pair of ballet slippers. Would you like to see those too, officer?" said Jennifer sarcastically.

"You weren't at dinner yesterday."

"So?"

"Why not?"

"My business to know and yours to find out."

"Look, Jennifer," said Clarice firmly, "your school and your teachers have got a lot to lose if we don't get that ring back to where it belongs. Why didn't you show for dinner?"

"I wasn't hungry."

Clarice frowned. "You mean to say that after that long day, and all that walking around the museum, you didn't feel hungry? I find that hard to believe."

"Look, I'm a dancer, okay? I have to be careful with my diet, and olive oil every day can be quite fattening." She shrugged. "I don't care if you believe it or not." She got up to go.

"Wait," said Clarice. "Where were you at dinnertime, in your room?"

"Bingo," said Jennifer.

"Did anyone see you there?"

"Maninder," said Jennifer over her shoulder as she moved fluidly away through the olive trees, back toward the ping-pong room. "Maninder's my room-mate. Thanks for the Coke, kids."

"Busybodies!" spluttered Sadie. "Kids!"

"Looks like Jennifer is not our Perp," said Clarice. "But check that alibi, Number Two, when you get a chance. Find out who Maninder is and ask her if Jennifer was in their room during and immediately after dinner yesterday. Now let's get out of this heat and go wash up for lunch."

Brick went off to his own room. The two girls lay on their beds in the cool of their room and listened to the hot clatter of the cicadas outside.

"Why did you examine Jennifer's sandals, Clarice?"

"Whoever smashed that exhibit case probably walked on broken glass. There were scratches on the cabinet under the escape window, remember?"

"So you were feeling for splinters embedded in the sole. That's pretty smart, Clarice."

The door burst open. Brick's scrawny body came leaping through, and landed in a crouch, facing their beds. His open hands slashed at the air. "Aieee!" he screamed.

"His fanbelt is slipping," said Sadie. "If he keeps it up his motor will burn out."

"Isn't it too hot for a frenzy, Number Three?" said Clarice.

"We should start keeping the door locked," said Sadie, "to keep crazies out."

The two girls yawned elaborately as they watched Brick practise a few silent high leg kicks and reverse heel blows on the hanging light fixture in the centre of the room before he slumped into the chair near the window. "What do we do next, Chief?"

Clarice examined her watch. "We eat." They went down to lunch.

 # Chapter 8

"This place gives me a headache," said Clarice.

They had been walking through the War Museum for only a few minutes, and already Clarice wanted out. "Old guns and helmets, grenades and medals! Who needs them!"

For once Sadie agreed. "Weapons are boring."

Mr. and Mrs. Stewart didn't seem to find it boring. They went cheerfully off on their own.

The three detectives sat down on a gun carriage.

"Weapons are for wimps," said Brick. "Fighting ought to be done with bare hands and feet." He sprang to his feet and flailed his hands and legs about and leaped into the air and crouched and leaped again. "Aiiieee!" he cried.

Clarice and Sadie ignored him. They were accustomed to Brick's sudden explosions of energy. What they were not accustomed to was this long speech. It was usually an effort for him to grunt.

Clarice said, "That's the most you've said on this whole trip, Number Three. The bowl of olives you ate with your lunch must have given you the gift of speech. But you're right. Bare hands would mean no bullets and bayonets."

"Just like Theseus," said Sadie to Brick, hoping to provoke him to further outbursts of speech.

But Brick only got up, scratched his spiky yellow head, and wandered off.

Sadie slipped off one of her sandals and examined her foot. "I don't know about bare hands, but I can see why Greek ruins are called ruins: walking around in sandals sure ruins your toenails."

"Toenails are not important," said Clarice. "Solving Crimes is important. Come on, let's find one of our Suspects."

They searched through the museum, and found Ann Furey with Max Darcy, sitting on the top of a battered World War II tank.

"Ann, we'd like to ask you a few questions," Clarice called up to her.

"Step aboard," Ann called down.

Sadie mounted the ladder behind Clarice.

"You can sit on the gun turret," said Max with a wave of his hand.

Ann moved to make room for them. The tall eighth grader was athletic-looking, with bright, alert eyes and a mass of curly black hair.

"Ann," said Clarice, "we're investigating the robbery of the gold ring from the museum. We think one of your group took it."

"Max told me you kids are detectives. Am I a suspect?" Ann smiled a friendly enough smile, but it was clear she thought this was all a childish game.

"Everyone's a suspect right now," said Clarice. "We don't have much to go on. We hope you can help us clear it up. If the police find — "

"You don't need to draw pictures for me," said Ann. "If the police find it's one of us, then Erin Lake Junior High is in trouble. I can see that all right."

"Do you believe the gold ring has supernatural powers?" said Clarice.

"No. I think *people* can have powers, but not things."

"Mind if we take a look at your sandals?"

"My sandals!" Ann laughed. "Are you serious?"

"The kiddycops must be looking for clues," Max said to Ann.

Sadie narrowed her eyes. With Ann around, Max had abandoned his charming manner and was treating even Clarice as a mild joke.

Ann slipped the sandals off her bare feet and handed them to Clarice. They were leather Birkenstocks.

"Why did you miss dinner yesterday, Ann?" said Clarice as she ran her hands lightly over the sandals.

Ann shrugged. "Wasn't hungry."

"Where were you?" pressed Clarice.

"I went to the Plaka to buy a T-shirt, one I've had my eye on."

"Did you leave the museum with the others when it closed at five?" said Clarice.

"Of course."

"So it would be about what time when you bought your T-shirt?"

"I dunno. Five-thirty maybe."

"Did anyone go with you?"

Ann shook her head. "I went alone."

"Did you tell your teachers you were going?"

Ann shook her head. "I skipped out."

"Aren't you supposed to tell them if you're not with the group?"

"I dared her to go," said Max with a sly smile.

"Dared her?" said Clarice. "Why?"

"It's called courting disaster," said Max. "If the Two Peas — "

"Two Peas?" said Clarice.

"That's what we call Miss Plum and Mr. Pollon," said Max with a laugh. "If they noticed Ann missing she'd be in trouble. But she can't resist a dare, can you, Ann?" Max's smile was sly and mocking.

Ann glared at Max, but said nothing.

"And did they notice you were missing?" said Clarice.

Ann made a face. "Yeah. They're going to be complaining to my parents when we get back, but — " She shrugged her shoulders.

Sadie decided again that she really didn't care much for Max Darcy. He had pushed Ann Furey into trouble.

Clarice handed Ann's sandals to Sadie who

started an intent examination, holding back her hair as she peered at the soles.

Max said, "I remember when Ann was in fourth grade and someone dared her to play a practical joke on Miss Binns — a strict old witch. So when Miss Binns confiscated two frogs that Ann had been having a conversation with on the top of her desk and put them in the stationery cupboard, Ann went out and collected — "

"I don't think they want to hear ancient history," said Ann coldly.

Max ignored her. " — collected a sackful of frogs from Erin Lake, got to school early the next morning, and released them into the cupboard. The rest is history, as they say. Miss Binns opened the cupboard during class to see what the noise was in there, and just about had a heart attack when all the little croakers came leaping out at her! You know what Ann said to Miss Binns? All the kids were howling. Ann yelled out above the noise, 'That's what happens, Miss, when you put two young frogs together in a dark cupboard!' The class broke up." Max laughed loudly and stamped his feet on the tank turret. "Another time, she rode her bike — "

"That's enough!" said Ann angrily. "You're

such a jerk sometimes, Max!"

Sadie handed the sandals back to Ann, who dropped them on the top of the tank and pushed her feet into them. "Well? Did you find what you were looking for?"

Clarice shrugged. Sadie said to Ann, "What happened to all the frogs?"

"The class helped me capture them all and return them to the pond."

Clarice stood, ready to go. "Do you have the gold ring, Ann?"

Ann shook her head, curls bouncing.

"I just hope we can find the ring soon," said Sadie, "otherwise all of you, and the Two Peas, will be in deep, deep trouble."

"Good luck, kiddycops!" said Max.

Clarice and Sadie climbed down off the tank. "I don't like Max Darcy," said Sadie. "What Ann sees in him I'll never know."

"Ann thinks we're funny," said Clarice, "thinks we're just elementary kids. But I like her."

"She's okay," agreed Sadie.

They found Brick near the exit with Sadie's mom and dad.

"We'll be outside, Mrs. Stewart," said Clarice. "Okay?"

Mrs. Stewart smiled. "Don't go too far away."

The three sleuths shouldered their way out the heavy revolving exit door into Monastiraki Square, and Clarice brought Brick up to date on the investigation. "Do you think Ann Furey took the ring, Chief?" said Brick.

"Too soon to say," said Clarice, "and there's no witness to her story. Sadie, did you follow up on Jennifer Hill's alibi?"

Sadie nodded. "Her room-mate is Maninder Manhas. Maninder says Jennifer was in their room. She didn't go down to dinner, but did some exercises and ate some fruit instead."

"So we can strike Jennifer the dancer off our list of suspects," said Clarice. "Which leaves Ann Furey, Kerry Krohn and Gloria Platt."

They meandered across the cobbled street and stopped to look in the window of a jewellery shop.

Brick walked into the shop. Clarice and Sadie followed. Brick picked up a ring from a tray on the counter, and handed it to Clarice. "Take a look at this, Chief."

Clarice examined the ring. Her titian eyebrows shot up in astonishment. She handed the ring to Sadie.

Sadie peered at the gold ring. It was perfect in every detail, right down to the man–bull design of the Minotaur. "It's exactly the same!" she exclaimed.

"A copy," said Clarice. She pointed to the 5000 drachma sign on the tray. "And obviously not real gold."

Sadie slipped the ring on her finger. It was too big. She reached into the tray and picked a smaller one. It was just right. The ring of the Minotaur! She had to have it. She held up her hand, admiring the ring. "What do you think?"

"Too expensive, Sadie," said Clarice. "That would be about forty dollars."

"No prob*lem,*" said Sadie, placing the accent on the second syllable as the Greeks did.

"But I thought you had only 1500 drachmas spending money left," said Clarice.

"Yes," said Sadie, "but that wasn't counting my emergency money."

"You didn't say anything about emergency money."

"Of course I didn't. If I told you I had it then it wouldn't be emergency money, would it? It would only be ordinary money."

Clarice frowned as she tried to follow her

friend's logic. She gave up. She turned to Brick. "Have you any idea what Number Two is talking about, Number Three?"

Brick shook his head.

"So how much money do you *really* have left?" said Clarice.

Sadie was still admiring the ring on her finger. "Oh, enough to buy this beautiful ring." She sighed happily. "Every time I look at it I'll remember Greece." She noticed Clarice frowning at her in a distinctly unfriendly way. "And I'll remember our wonderful friendship, exploring Greece together, solving the case of the gold ring, the three musketeers, all for one and one for all."

Clarice's expression lightened. "Well, the ring does look good on you, Sadie. And you don't have a ring." She held up her own hand. "I bought my yin–yang ring last Easter in Horsefly when I visited my Aunt Esther and my cousin, Moonflower." She turned to show it to Brick but he had moved away to the opposite counter and was examining another tray of jewellery.

The two girls wandered around the shop admiring the brooches and necklaces. When they looked around again for Brick he had disappeared. They were not concerned. His comings and goings were often erratic.

Sadie paid for her ring and they strolled back across the street to the War Museum. Sadie couldn't stop admiring her ring.

They sat on the steps, near the waiting bus, and soon Mr. and Mrs. Stewart came out of the museum. Sadie showed them her new ring.

The Lakers emerged from the museum.

There was no sign of Brick.

"There he is," said Clarice, pointing up to the back of the bus. Brick was asleep in the rear seat. Clarice and Sadie moved closer. They stared at a flash of silver. "It's an earring," said Sadie.

Dangling from a thin silver chain on Brick's ear was a tiny silver Minotaur.

 # Chapter 9

Only a short bus ride from Athens along the scenic coast road, the Temple of Poseidon at Cape Sounion stands high above the sparkling Aegean Sea. The cliffs there are steep and dangerous.

Mr. and Mrs. Stewart had accepted the invitation from Miss Plum to accompany their three charges on the Lakers' bus tour to the temple. It was now early evening and, although the sun hung lower in the blue sky, it was still hot. Everyone took frequent swallows from their water bottles. The detectives stood looking out to sea, their backs to the sixteen graceful Doric columns of the temple. A hundred metres beneath their feet, the surf boiled around jagged black rocks.

Sadie said, "This is the place where Theseus' father, King Aegeus, threw himself into the sea."

"Here?" said Brick. "Really?"

"That's why the sea is named after him," said Sadie.

"You mean he killed himself?" said Clarice. "Why did he do that?"

"He thought the Minotaur had killed and eaten his son, Prince Theseus. Crazed with grief, he hurled himself over." Sadie pointed. "Right at this very spot."

Clarice peered over the edge of the cliff. The waves crashed with a roar on the rocks below. The wind pulled at her hat. Some of the other kids were yelling and shouting as they chased their hats around Poseidon's Temple.

"You realize that this is our very last full day in Greece, don't you," said Clarice.

Brick nodded his head.

Sadie said, "The time goes too fast."

"Come on. We've got to make Kerry and Gloria give us some hard answers," said Clarice, holding on to her hat. They made their way along the edge of the cliff.

Sadie stopped, listening. "What was that?"

"What was what?" said Clarice.

"Sounded like a cry for help."

"You're hearing things," said Clarice. "Probably the wind."

"There it is again," said Sadie, her slightly prominent ears pointed towards the edge of the cliff like radio antennas.

Clarice and Brick stood and listened. "A seagull," said Clarice, "or one of the kids chasing through the ruins."

"There it is again!" said Sadie. "It's coming from the cliff over on the other side!" Sadie hurried toward the end of the temple. Clarice and Brick followed. Sadie ran on past the temple, and came to a halt on a high bluff.

"Look!" Sadie pointed down the hill.

Kerry Krohn was lying on his stomach at the edge of the cliff, reaching down over the cliff with both arms.

"Help!" came a faint cry.

"Come on!" Clarice swept off her sunhat and, waving it aloft like a flag, charged down the slope, skipping and running and jumping over sod and rock, her hair flying out behind her.

Sadie and Brick followed. "Wait for me!" cried

Sadie as she tried to keep up with her faster friends. When she got there, Sadie could see that Kerry was lying stretched out on the edge where a small patch of clay and sod had collapsed and dropped into the sea far below.

"Help me!" Kerry gasped.

The detectives lay on their stomachs and peered nervously over the cliff edge.

On a narrow rocky ledge a metre and a half down, one hand grasping Kerry's outstretched hand and his other arm clinging to a stunted tree, was Max Darcy, his dark eyes wide with terror.

"Hold on, Max!" yelled Clarice. "We'll get you."

Brick reached a hand down to the terrified boy. "Chief," yelled Brick, "hang on to my ankles."

Clarice lay down on the grass behind Brick and grabbed onto his ankles. Sadie did the same with Kerry. The wind swept Sadie's hat from her head and sent it sailing away over the cliff.

"Let go of the tree," Brick shouted down to Max, "and grab my hand."

But Max was too scared to release his hold on the tree. "I can't," he cried.

"Do it!" yelled Kerry. "We can pull you up."

Max released his hold on the tree and frantically grabbed Brick's outstretched hand. Brick held on tight. Now Brick and Kerry started hauling Max up slowly. "Pull!" gasped Kerry.

"Aieee!" cried Brick, pulling with all his strength.

Max came up over the edge and pitched forward onto the grass. Brick and Kerry fell backwards.

"Saved!" sighed Clarice.

"Phew!" said Sadie.

Max Darcy lay trembling on the grass in the long shadows of Poseidon's Temple.

Kerry got up. He wiped his brow. "It was an accident. Part of the cliff collapsed."

"You shoved me!" said Max angrily. His face was white.

"I didn't shove you!" said Kerry with a sneer. "If you hadn't swung at me — " He stopped.

"What were you arguing about?" said Clarice.

Kerry did not answer. He took a last contemptuous look at Max Darcy, still lying on the grass, then headed away up the hill toward the temple without another word.

Clarice knelt on one knee beside Max. "You

okay?" She took his arm to help him up, but he shook it off and climbed unsteadily to his feet. "What were you fighting about, Max?"

"None of your business, kid," said Max, turning and limping away.

Sadie's mouth dropped open. "The ungrateful swine! We practically saved his life!"

Clarice said, "We *did* save his life, all of us, Kerry too. If you hadn't heard his cry for help, Sadie — "

"He'd be dead," said Sadie with a shiver as she peered over the cliff at the pounding ocean far below.

Chapter 10

The setting sun cast its last rays through the narrow cobbled streets of the Plaka, painting the white walls of the Hermes Taverna orange and gold.

Sadie had persuaded her mom and dad to dine at the Hermes because the Lakers were coming here. It was the Lakers' final evening in Athens also. "It will probably be our last chance to question Kerry and Gloria," said Clarice.

The three sleuths and Sadie's parents chose an outdoor table for dinner, and had no sooner settled themselves with the water the waiter brought when the Lakers arrived, causing a minor commotion as they found tables.

"Can you see where Kerry Krohn is sitting?" Clarice whispered.

Brick pointed. Sadie and Clarice saw the wiry thirteen-year-old sitting with Gloria Platt at a table for two. Kerry looked around quickly to see if anyone was watching, then leaned over and gave Gloria a kiss.

"Yuck! I don't ever want to kiss a boy!" said Sadie.

"Me neither," said Brick.

"Oh, I don't know," said Clarice. "It couldn't be any worse than being kissed by my Aunt Esther and her mustache."

"Mom, would it be okay if we sat over there on our own?" said Sadie.

Mrs. Stewart smiled and nodded.

Three men were dancing to the music of a bouzouki in the café across the street. Arms around each other's shoulders, eyes closed, the two at the ends with their arms stretched out wide, fingers snapping, they seemed in a trance.

Brick got up from the table, ambled across the street into the café, looped one arm around the shoulders of one of the men, and began dancing. He moved with the men, lightly, gracefully, his free arm floating, fingers snapping.

"Will you look at that!" said Sadie. She watched Brick in astonishment. He seemed to change right before her eyes: one minute he was a thin eleven-year-old, and the next he was ageless, dancing, swaying, with music crackling from his hair and fingers.

"I don't know about Jennifer Hill," said Clarice, "but Number Three could be a world-famous dancer some day."

After several minutes, the bouzouki music reached a crescendo. The four dancers gave a leap on one foot, raised their right knees, then squatted, and gave a final leap high in the air as the music ended. The crowd cheered. The three men shook Brick's hands and clapped him enthusiastically on the back.

Brick ambled back, his face flushed, and sat down, a boy once more.

"Great stuff, kid!" Gloria Platt called from the next table.

"Well done, Number Three," said Clarice.

Sadie was still too astonished to say anything.

"*Kefi*," said Brick.

"Not for me, thanks," said Sadie, finding her voice. "I don't like coffee."

Brick shook his spiky yellow head. "*Kefi*.It's Greek. It means feeling good."

"I don't think any of us will have *kefi* until this whole ring business is settled," said Clarice. "Let's move our table over a little so we can talk to Kerry and Gloria."

They moved their table.

"That was great dancing," said Kerry to Brick.

"Thanks."

Clarice said, "You were pretty great yourself, grabbing Max Darcy like that. You saved his life."

Kerry shrugged. "The guy's an idiot. He was lucky you kids were there to help."

"You want to tell us what you were arguing about?" said Clarice.

Kerry shook his head. "It was nothing." He waved a hand dismissively.

Gloria nodded. "Kerry's right. Darcy's a jerk."

"Why did you two miss dinner yesterday?" asked Clarice.

Kerry snorted. "Are you kids working for the Greek FBI?"

Gloria gave a high-pitched, one-note laugh. Sadie glared at her.

"Where were you both yesterday when the museum alarm went off?" Clarice persisted.

Kerry held up his hands. "I surrender, I surrender. If I answer your questions, will you leave us alone?" At a nod from Clarice, he lowered his arms and took a sip from his water glass. "We didn't hear the alarm," he said. "After we got out of the museum we snuck along to the Plaka for a couple of Cokes and a smoke. You can never sneak a smoke with the Two Peas always watching you."

"Cigarettes are carcinogenic," said Sadie.

"So live dangerously," said Gloria with a sneer.

"You missed dinner," said Clarice.

"That's right," said Kerry. "We were late getting back because of the crowds in the Plaka. The streets were jammed tight. Must have been something special going on. When the Two Peas asked why we weren't at dinner I told them we weren't hungry." He grinned. "Which was true. We pigged out on those great coconut bars you get in the Plaka."

"And that's all you know?" said Clarice.

Kerry nodded. "That's it."

"You seemed very interested in the gold ring

just before the museum closed," said Clarice.

"It wasn't the ring, it was the skeleton I liked the best," said Kerry.

"Could we see your sandals?" said Clarice.

"You want to see sandals?" squeaked Kerry.

"I told you these kids were a bit bent," said Gloria through her chewing gum.

"It will help our investigation a lot if you let us check your sandals," said Clarice.

"There's no way I'm taking off my sandals in this place," said Gloria. "You're gonna need a search warrant."

Kerry wore rubber thongs. He kicked them toward Clarice. "You can look at mine if you want. While you're at it, check under the hood and wipe the windows. Ha!"

Gloria snickered.

Clarice examined the thongs and handed them back to Kerry. "Sure you don't want to change your mind?" she said to Gloria.

"Oh, take them," said Gloria, kicking off her leather sandals. "You won't find anything."

Clarice checked the sandals carefully, and then gave them back.

"Why don't you kids move your table back so we can get some privacy," said Gloria.

"What were you and Max arguing about?" said Clarice again.

"No comment," said Kerry. "Now get."

The detectives moved their table back and sat in silence watching the dancers across the street while they waited for their food to come. A line of five men had started dancing together, arms around each others shoulders. The bouzouki music was loud and dramatic. The men swayed and bobbed like the sea, ebbing and flowing, their eyes closed in mystical concentration.

"*Kefi*," said Brick.

* * *

"I think Kerry is the thief," said Sadie.

"What about Gloria?" said Clarice.

"I can't see Gloria leaping over that high fence," said Sadie, "even with the help of the magic ring, can you?"

The detectives trudged up the hotel stairs. Sadie was tired. It had been a long day. The moon shone in the window, making the room bright. Clarice did not switch on the light. Brick lay on the rug, Clarice sat on her bed with her back against the wall. From the way Clarice was staring into space and tapping her lower lip with one of the hotel pencils, Sadie could tell that she was thinking hard. Sadie fingered her new ring and looked out at the moonlit Agora and the Acropolis. She yawned. "We've questioned all the suspects: Jennifer Hill, Ann Furey, Kerry Krohn and Gloria Platt, and we've come up with nothing. A big fat zero."

"What time is our flight tomorrow, Number Two?"

"Two o'clock."

"We've *got* to get the ring back by tomorrow morning," said Clarice. "It's our last chance."

"Maybe we should tell the Two Peas all we know and let them try to sort it out," said Sadie.

"That won't be necessary," said Clarice. "I feel confident that the Solution to the Crime is very close."

"You know who the thief — the Perp — is?" said Sadie in surprise.

"I've got a Hunch," said Clarice, "that's all."

"Who is it, Chief?"

"Well, I don't think it's Kerry or Gloria."

"Why not?" said Sadie.

"They were in the Plaka when the robbery was being committed," said Clarice.

"But why should we believe them?" said Sadie. "There were no witnesses who saw them there."

"No," said Clarice, "but if they had *not* been in the Plaka, then they wouldn't have known how unusually crowded it was at that time."

"But they could have made that up," protested Sadie.

Clarice shook her head. "They were telling the truth. The Plaka was crowded because of a big anti-government rally. There were speeches and people marching."

"How do you know all this?" said Sadie.

"I saw it on the front page of Mr. Pappas' paper. There was a picture of a man shaking his fist at one of the speakers. I wondered if it might have something to do with the stolen ring, so I asked Mr. Pappas and he told me it was a political rally."

Sadie said, "So they *were* telling the truth. Hmmph! Jennifer Hill's got an alibi, so that leaves only Ann Furey, who skipped out to the Plaka on a dare to buy a T-shirt."

"Looks that way," said Clarice.

"We should ask Ann whether the Plaka was crowded," said Sadie. "If she was lying about her shopping trip then she probably wouldn't know about the crowds."

"We can ask her a few Incisive Questions tomorrow," agreed Clarice. She glanced at her wristwatch. "Let's get to bed. We've got to try and get that ring back to the museum tomorrow morning. There's nothing more going to happen tonight."

But Clarice was wrong. She didn't know it, but the night was far from over.

 **Chapter 11**

A full silver moon hung over the Acropolis; the night air shimmered with silent expectancy as a curling breeze lifted the thin curtains of the girls' bedroom and wafted a sweet smell of sandalwood and sage and ancient marble into their warm, untroubled sleep.

Sadie was unable to say afterwards what it was that woke her up: the smells, the silver bars of moonlight lying heavily across her bed perhaps, or the hoot of the goddess Athena's favourite bird, the owl, in the Agora. Whatever it was, she felt compelled to fumble her glasses on and tiptoe over to the open window to look out.

The treed courtyard was all moonlight and shadows. Sadie contentedly breathed in the perfumed night air. She leaned her forearms on the sill. The tall columns of Vulcan's temple were black against the purple of the night. Moonlight edged the temple's ancient pediment with silver.

She looked at her watch. Exactly midnight.

She thought again of the Minotaur, and allowed her fancy to roam down through the dark, damp passageways of the Labyrinth, seeing in her imagination the lonely imprisoned monster hidden away from all eyes. She felt sorry for the monster; after all, was it his fault he had been born with the head of a bull? No, the fault lay with his parents, who had angered the gods. Nor was it his fault that he had to devour human flesh: it was his nature, and he could not escape what was natural to him.

Across the roadway in the ancient burial ground, moonlight and shadows created strange, fantastic shapes among granite and marble tombstones and fluted columns. Wasn't that the Minotaur himself she could see lurking in the shadows? His great bull head raised high, sighing in the graveyard? No, it was only a cypress stirring in the breeze.

She relaxed. Then she thought she saw something moving. Probably a cat. There were cats everywhere in Athens. Sadie stared down, alert, listening. Sadie was proud of her sensitive ears. If there was anything down there moving about, then she would hear it.

There was only the night breezes in the olive trees. But wait! She could hear something moving in the silence, something trembling in the graveyard across the road, something sibilant and whispery in the silvery moonlight! Sadie's eyes widened behind her glasses. She stared, waiting. It came again: a rustle of leaves, a slight movement near a tall, moonlit headstone.

Sadie felt her heart quicken. What could it be? A god or goddess? A ghost of Ancient Greece — a king or queen or hero? Perhaps it *was* the Minotaur, or Theseus himself, restlessly seeking the gold ring that was rightfully his, snatched from his grave, and now stolen from the museum!

She scrambled over to Clarice's bed and shook her friend awake. "Clarice, quick!"

Clarice sat up, rubbing her eyes.

"Look out the window!" Sadie pointed out

toward the graveyard. "There's something out there!"

Still half asleep, Clarice stumbled over to the window.

"A god from Mount Olympus!" said Sadie, her voice hoarse with excitement. "Or a ghost!"

Clarice stared. "You had too much sun today, Sadie! It's gone to your head."

"Look! Over there! Something moved!"

"You've got to stop pouring so much vinegar on your salad; it's starting to pickle your brains."

"Look at that spot near the cypress! Behind the tombstone! Something's moving!"

Clarice stared. "You're right, there's someone there. Sandals on and let's go!"

"What! Like this? In our PJs?"

But Clarice had slipped into her sandals and was already out the door. Sadie grabbed her sandals and scrambled after her, down the stairs, and through the rustling, silver-coated olive trees in the courtyard.

"What the — !" Clarice stumbled and fell over a body lying under a tree. The body leaped up. The two girls fell back in fright.

The moonlight lit up the face. It was Brick in shorts and T-shirt.

Clarice lost her temper. "What do you think you're doing, Number Three! You scared us half to death!"

Brick grinned. "Sorry, Chief. What's up?"

"Follow us!" said Clarice.

"Be quiet," said Sadie. She knew it was no good asking Brick why he had been sleeping outside under the olive trees in the moonlight; Brick operated under laws peculiarly his own, and if questioned would merely grin and shrug his thin shoulders.

They hurried across the road to the graveyard. The entrance, a tall, spiked wrought iron gate, was impassable, but the walls were broken and crumbled in places, leaving gaps. The moon lighting their way, the three detectives clambered over the wall, trying not to make any noise, and dropped down onto broken fragments of nameless tombstones half buried amongst vines and weeds and crabgrass.

Sadie's heart pounded, not from the dash down the hotel stairs and the shock of running into Brick, but from fear pure and simple. It was the middle of the night, and here she was, creeping through ancient gravestones. It didn't matter that most of the graves had been opened and robbed eons ago; that there probably remained nothing but a splinter or two of human bone buried deep under the worn and shattered slabs. If anything, an empty graveyard seemed even more scary than one full of freshly buried corpses. Sadie shivered with fright.

Clarice led the way past a cracked and leaning Doric column toward the cypress tree where they had seen movement. Sadie and Brick followed, silently picking their way through toppled and half-sunken gravestones. An owl hooted down at them like a trumpet of doom and they froze like statues. Even Brick underwent a startling transformation as his mouth fell open in a strangled gasp and his spiky yellow hair stood up even more stiffly from his scalp.

"Shhh!" whispered Clarice, the first to recover.

They moved forward slowly. As they drew close to the tall cypress, the moon disappeared behind a cloud. They stopped. Sadie could see nothing. Alone and adrift in the darkness, trembling, she reached out and hung onto a gravestone as though it were a lifebuoy in a black and faceless sea. "Clarice!" she whispered. The gravestone was covered in ivy. What if the vines clung to her and dragged her down into the grave? She jerked her hand away with a small cry, then slipped and fell on her knees.

"Ouch!" she cried as the rough eroded stone scraped the skin from her knees.

"Sadie! Are you all right?" Clarice bent over her in the thick darkness and helped her to her feet.

The moon came out again, luminous and restoring. Sadie rubbed her injured knees and took a deep breath to relieve the pain.

"You okay?" said Clarice.

Out of the corner of her eye, Sadie saw a flash of brightness up ahead. There was someone behind the cypress, someone in a white, floating garment that glowed in the moonlight. "A ghost!" breathed Sadie. Her glasses slid down to the end of her nose in astonishment.

The three detectives crowded together behind a tombstone and stared, trying to adjust their eyes to the brightness in front of them. "It's coming towards us!" whispered Sadie as the bright figure advanced.

"No it's not," whispered Clarice. "It stopped in the shadows. Look!" She pointed. "There's someone else moving over on the other side, see?"

Sadie adjusted her glasses. At first, she could see only black shadows and the ragged bars of moonlight through the graveyard. Then she saw a second, darker figure emerge from the darkness and approach the shadows where the white ghost stood waiting. Voices, whispering voices, sibilant and terrifying, plotting, Sadie was sure, to carry her away.

"It's two kids!" whispered Clarice.

Kids. Not ghosts. Sadie stared. The two figures moved from the shadows into the moonlight. Clarice was right: there were two kids, one dressed in a flowing white robe. The murmur of voices came more clearly.

"What are they saying, Number Two?" said Clarice in a hoarse whisper.

But Sadie could not stop trembling long enough to reply.

"Where's that so-called powerful hearing of yours?" demanded Clarice.

Sadie tried to concentrate. Clarice and Brick depended on her superior hearing powers. She pushed her hair back from her ears, tried to listen, tried to still the wild beat of her heart and stop the trembling in her knees. The murmurs grew more distinct. Two kids, a boy and a girl, their droning voices amplified and distorted amidst the marble stones and broken columns. Sadie tried to concentrate on the words.

" . . . dare . . . graveyard . . . " A boy's voice.

The girl spoke sharply to him. Sadie relaxed. The words began to come through. "I gave you a scare, admit it!" said the girl.

"So you spooked the heck out of me," said the boy. "But I should have guessed you'd dress up as a ghost; you're crazy enough to do anything."

The voices had a familiar lilt to Sadie's ears, but she couldn't identify their owners; shattered against the moonlit marble, the voices lost much of their unique colour and timbre.

"This is your last chance," said the girl. "If you don't give me the ring I go to the police."

The voices stopped.

"They're talking about the ring," Sadie whispered to Clarice.

"Duck down!" said Clarice. "They're coming this way."

"You want I should grab them, Chief?" whispered Brick.

Clarice nodded her head. "The boy."

The three sleuths crouched and huddled together behind the headstone as the two figures came closer. Sadie could see them clearly in the bright moonlight. When they were close enough to touch, Clarice leaped out on them. Brick grabbed the boy.

"What the . . . " yelped Ann Furey.

"Take your filthy hands off me!" snarled Max Darcy.

 **Chapter 12**

Max Darcy pulled away and threw a punch at Brick. Brick dodged it easily, and kicked Max's legs from under him. Max fell with a loud cry. He crouched, snarling, ready to attack once again.

"Hold it right there, Max," said Clarice. "The game's up. We know you've got the ring."

Max Darcy stood and brushed the dirt off his arms, his face livid with rage. "You don't know anything!" he spat. Then he turned and ran. Brick went after him.

The two boys ran through the graveyard, dodging around trees and bushes and jumping over tombstones. Max was fast and tricky on his feet. Brick was fast also, but could not shorten the distance between himself and the older boy. Sadie had never before seen anyone who could outrun Brick. Perhaps Max has the ring on him, she thought.

Sadie heard Brick utter a high-pitched cry like the night call of an alley cat. A small army of cats appeared, screeching and shrieking about Max's flashing feet.

Max tripped over the swarming cats and fell heavily to the ground.

Brick cried again and leaped onto Max's back. The cats disappeared as suddenly as they had come.

Brick hung onto Max, his arms looped around the bigger boy's neck from behind in a half nelson. Max yelled and resisted, but he could not escape Brick's tight grip. Clarice, Sadie and Ann advanced on the writhing pair.

Max's struggles were growing weaker. "I give in," he choked. "You got me."

"The ring!" said Clarice.

"Hand it over, Max," said Ann.

"I don't have it!"

"Yes, you do," said Ann. She reached into the

pocket of Max's shorts, took out the gold ring, and handed it to Clarice.

"Phew!" Brick released his prisoner and sat back against a marble slab, wiping his brow.

Clarice examined the ring closely, then passed it to Sadie. Sadie ran her thumb over the engraved Minotaur and compared the real ring with her own. Her blood tingled in her fingers and arms. She didn't want to let the real ring go. The gold ring of Theseus! She was holding it in her hands! She felt the excitement deep in her bones, and for a while she forgot to breathe.

Clarice said gently, "Sadie?"

Sadie reluctantly passed the ring to Brick, who held up the glittering ring and examined the engraving closely. Sadie thought his eyes glinted gold in the moonlight like the ring in his hand. He rubbed the Minotaur gently with his finger, then handed the ring back to Clarice.

Sadie said to Clarice, "But how could Max have done it? He sat with us at dinner, remember? He couldn't have been in the museum at the time the ring was being stolen!"

"Max knew the thief was in the museum," said Clarice. She turned to Ann. "Ann stole it, didn't you, Ann? Max dared you to. Just as he

dared you to meet him tonight in the graveyard."

Ann nodded. Her eyes flashed. "That's right,
he dared me! I was a fool. I gave him the ring to
prove I'd stolen it, but he wouldn't give it back."

Clarice said to Max. "Ann gave you the ring
expecting you to return it to the museum. What
happened? Changed your mind when you got it
in your greedy hands? Or did you plan to keep it
from the start?"

Max Darcy said nothing.

"We've got to return this ring, Max," continued Clarice. "I only hope it isn't too late. You
were crazy to think you could keep it! Why would
you risk a Greek jail? Why would you risk involv-
ing your school and your teachers in a scandal?
All for this ring! Why?"

Max stared down at his feet, his face white in
the moonlight, his fists clenched.

Sadie said, "You think it has special powers,
right?"

Still Max said nothing.

"Is that it?" asked Clarice. "You want to be a
hero? You want people to look up to you?"

Max kept his eyes down, staring at the
ground.

Ann said, "You don't need the ring, Max. You're the best athlete Erin Lake ever had. You shine at everything — football, soccer, basketball . . . "

Max stared wildly at Ann. "But you don't know what it's like! Every time I play I feel the pressure. What if I don't play well? What if I let everyone down? Having the ring made me feel confident and strong. The ring would keep me from failing."

Ann shook her head. "The only thing the ring does is make you dishonest. Winning is fine, but what about self-respect?"

"*Philotimo,*" said Brick.

"What's *philotimo?*" said Sadie.

"Self-respect. Pride," said Brick. "Very important to Greeks."

Max looked down at the ground again. Ann wrapped her long, flowing ghost disguise about her waist to get it out of the way. "How did you know it was me who stole the ring?" she asked Clarice.

"Your sandals gave you away," said Clarice.

Ann said, "They couldn't have. I knew you were looking for glass in the soles. I thought of that earlier, and dug out every tiny bit. Took me ages. By the time you looked there wasn't a sliver left in them."

Clarice said, "No glass, but the leather had soaked up so much water it was still damp."

Sadie said, "They were a bit damp, Clarice, but what does that prove?"

Clarice said, "The thief hid in the amphora waiting for the museum to close and all the guards to leave. Don't you remember, Number Two, how you had to dry yours out after you'd been in the water jar? You stood in the water for only a few minutes. Ann must have stood in there for an hour."

"I didn't think of that," admitted Sadie.

"Good work, Chief," said Brick.

Ann nodded. "Very clever of you, Clarice. I did hide in the jar. It was wet all right."

Clarice shrugged modestly. "You also gave yourself away with your story about shopping for a T-shirt, Ann. You said you bought the shirt about five-thirty, when everyone knows the shops in the Plaka close for a siesta between two and six. Especially yesterday during the political rally."

Ann threw back her head and laughed. "You'll be a world-famous detective some day, Clarice,

I'm sure of it. You're absolutely right: there was no T-shirt. And yes, I did steal the ring." She took a deep breath. "Stealing it was scary. But I enjoyed it. I enjoyed the thrill of getting away with it, I guess. But I'd no intention of keeping it. I wanted to return it right away, but — " she glared at Max, " — he wouldn't give it back. I almost told you that Max had the ring when you were examining my sandals on top of the tank, and Max was being oh-so-smart telling you he'd dared me to cut out and go shopping. But I thought I'd be able to persuade him to return it, I really did."

Max glared at Ann. He was slumped against a gravestone. The moonlight was so bright Sadie could see where Max had scraped his cheek in the chase and drawn a little blood.

"I think Kerry Krohn knew about Max having the ring," said Clarice. "I don't know how he found out — "

Ann said, "Max showed it to him. He couldn't help bragging that he had it."

"Which is probably why they were arguing," said Clarice. "Kerry wanted you to return it, didn't he, Max?"

Max shrugged.

Sadie said, "That ring almost cost you your life, Max."

"You can thank Sadie's ears you're not dead," said Clarice.

"I'll take the ring to the police," said Ann.

"That might not be a wise move, Ann," said Clarice. "Why not simply let us put it in an envelope and we can drop it into a mailbox?"

"I was going to do that," said Ann, "but I've changed my mind. I wanted to impress Max. I liked him. I wanted us to be friends. But stealing a ring on a dare was the wrong way to do it." She was silent for a while, then she looked at Brick. "I guess I could use some of that *philotimo* myself."

Ann turned to Clarice. "Now I must dare myself to face the police. You're all welcome to come with me to the police station." She gave a wan smile and held out her hand to Clarice for the ring.

Clarice looked at Sadie and Brick. They nodded. Clarice handed Ann the ring.

"*Efcharistó*," said Ann, smiling at the three detectives.

She gathered her ghostly garment about her, made her way through the gap in the broken wall and strode off along the narrow street that led to the police station.

The three detectives followed.

 **Chapter 13**

Clarice, Sadie and Brick were silent as they followed behind Ann through the twisting Plaka streets, leaving Max behind to make his own way back to the hotel. After a while Clarice said, "That was good work, Number Three."

"Thanks, Chief."

"You too, Number Two," said Clarice.

"Thanks," said Sadie. "You were pretty good yourself."

"Max had us fooled," said Clarice. "He always came across as Mr. Confidence."

"But he wasn't very confident at all," agreed Sadie. "You can never tell with people."

When they reached the police station they

stood outside in the street for a minute. Clarice said, "Leave the ring in the mail slot, Ann. Then the whole business will be over and done with."

Ann shook her head stubbornly. "I need to do this the hard way."

Clarice said, "Are you sure this isn't just another daring game for you, Ann?"

"Yeah, maybe it is," said Ann. "But this time I'm daring myself, and that's different."

"Even if it means you might be thrown in jail?" said Sadie.

"It's not a dare if there's no risk involved, is it?" Ann turned, straightened her shoulders, and with the layers of white sheet wrapped tightly about her, marched into the police station. The three detectives followed.

There was only one man inside. He was sitting at a desk reading a newspaper. He put the paper down as Ann approached. "Here," said Ann. She thrust out her arm and handed the ring to the policeman.

The policeman took the ring. He looked at it. Then he looked at Ann, and at Brick and the pyjama-clad Clarice and Sadie behind her. He waited for them to speak.

Ann said, "Do you speak English?"

The policeman nodded his head. "A little." He was a calm, quiet man, with a slow deliberate way of speaking. He had the usual black mustache and bushy grey hair. The small sign on the desk said "N. Stavros."

Ann said, "Officer Stavros, the ring you hold in your hand is the gold ring stolen from the museum. I'm returning it."

Officer Stavros said nothing. He merely raised his bushy eyebrows and carefully placed the ring on the green blotter on the top of the desk in front of him, examining it for several seconds without touching it. Then he looked up at Ann, his face very serious. "Your name?"

"Ann Furey."

"Your friends?" He jerked his chin at the detectives.

"They had nothing to do with it," said Ann. "I'm the one responsible. Tomorrow we return home to Canada."

"You could have returned this," Officer Stavros waved a hand at the ring, "in the mail to the museum, and tomorrow you would be gone." He lifted one shoulder. "Why you do this?"

"Because," said Ann, "because I want to be up front — "

"Upfront?"

"I wanted to come clean."

"Come clean?" Officer Stavros shook his head in puzzlement.

"*Philotimo*," said Ann.

"Ah!" Officer Stavros nodded solemnly.

"I'm sorry I caused this trouble," said Ann.

Officer Stavros studied Ann's tense, pale face, his brows drawn together in a frown. He said nothing for a while. Then, "You all stay at Ariadne Hotel, yes?"

"That's right," said Ann.

Officer Stavros picked up the ring and held it up to the light. "Is very beautiful, yes?"

"Yes, sir," said Ann.

The policeman said, "Sacred gold ring of Minos is treasure of my country. It tells about our history and our people." He paused, thinking. Then, "Many have taken away from my country the treasures like this one. They do not bring them back. Thank you for bringing this back." He smiled. "You are brave girl to come here. So I will tell you the little secret. Real gold ring of Minos is kept in safe with other such treasures."

Ann and the three detectives let out a

combined gasp of astonishment.

Ann said, "You mean — "

The policeman nodded his head slowly. "This is the clever copy. Is only the gold plating. Can be purchased in any jewellery shop for a few thousand drachmas, you understand?" He pointed to the ring on Sadie's finger. "Like so. Many important treasures are copied. The gold mask of Agamemnon is another such copy. Original mask is kept in secret place."

"Are you going to arrest me?" said Ann.

Officer Stavros shook his head. "Not this time." He smiled. "Have the safe trip home."

"*Efcharistó*, Officer Stavros," said Ann.

When they were once again outside in the street, Sadie said, "That *was* very brave of you, Ann."

"Good work, Ann," said Clarice.

Ann gave a happy grin. "Thanks."

Sadie said, "We should have guessed the ring was a phony. The Greeks are too smart to allow anyone to rob them."

They made their way around the fence, back to the hotel, no longer silent but talkative and happy. They crowded the hotel lobby with their boisterous good spirits. Only Aphrodite was on desk duty; she stretched out her neck for a touch from Brick.

They pushed fifty-drachma coins into the hotel lobby pop machine and toasted one another, holding their bottles high in triumph. "Cheers!" said Clarice.

Mr. Pappas appeared in a bright red dressing gown. Before he could say anything, Sadie handed him a bottle of Coke. "Mr. Pappas," she said, "we are celebrating." She raised her bottle high. "Here's to the wonderful country of Greece!"

Mr. Pappas smiled. "I propose the toast to Canada!"

The others cheered. The noise brought out other Lakers who rattled coins into the pop machine and joined in the celebration.

Mr. and Mrs. Stewart appeared, their faces puffed with sleep.

"Hi, Mom, Dad," said Sadie. "We're just saying goodbye. Here, have some Coke."

Max Darcy stood in the doorway of the dingy room, watching. Then he shouldered his way over to the pop machine and got himself a Coke.

Soon Miss Plum and Mr. Pollon were also in their midst, smiling and happy at this unplanned and unexpected leave-taking. Several other hotel guests joined the revelry. Mr. Pappas repeated his toast to Canada, and Sadie repeated hers to Greece.

Ann Furey held her bottle high. "Here's to our friends from British Columbia!"

Sadie's parents beamed.

"Here's to our friends from Ontario!" said Sadie.

Mr. Pollon proposed a toast to Mr. Pappas and the Ariadne Hotel. Miss Plum proposed a toast to Erin Lake School, and congratulated the children on their excellent behaviour and cheerfulness during their tour of Greece. As soon as she suggested the band get their instruments so they could play a celebratory march, the party suddenly and quickly broke up.

Upstairs in their room, Clarice lay on her bed. Sadie sat by the window looking at the Greek moon for the last time.

Clarice said, "Another Case Solved, Sadie."

"Another case solved," agreed Sadie.

Clarice switched off her bedside light and climbed between the covers. "Go to bed, Sadie," she said. "It's a long day's journey home tomorrow."

"I'm too excited to sleep. Our last night in Greece." Sadie sighed. "I want to remember it forever, I want to hold it all, I don't want to let any of it go."

"Sadie?"

"Hmmmnn?"

"That Theseus story you told us?"

"What about it?"

"I read it in your myth book."

"You did?"

"It wasn't quite the same story as the one you told."

"Oh?"

"There was nothing in the book about any gold ring. And nothing about compassion and Theseus calling the Minotaur 'poor monster.' There was no conversation between Theseus and the monster at all! And nothing about the Minotaur saying thanks just before he died. You made all that up."

Sadie was silent. Then she said, "Maybe I did. But everything I said was true."

Silence.

"Sadie?"

"Hmmnn?"

"I like your version better."

"Thanks."

"You never really finished telling it, you know," said Clarice sleepily.

"Yes I did."

"Didn't." Clarice yawned. "You didn't tell if Theseus got out of the Labyrinth with the other teenagers, and you didn't tell if Ariadne was waiting for him."

"Oh, they got out all right. They followed the twine back to the entrance. And yes, Ariadne was waiting to throw her arms around Theseus and take care of his wounds. He told her he had killed the Minotaur, and she wept with happiness that he was back safe in her arms."

Clarice was almost asleep. "And they lived happily ever after?"

"Not really," murmured Sadie. "Not everyone in a Greek story lives happily ever after."

James Heneghan is a retired school teacher — *and* a former police officer, fingerprint expert and photographer. Whether in the classroom or on the streets, his experience in crime gives him lots of ideas for mystery writing!

He lives in British Columbia, close to the famous Stanley Park. He has written *Blue, The Case of the Marmalade Cat, The Trail of the Chocolate Thief* and (with Bruce McBay as "B.J. Bond") *Goodbye, Carleton High*, all for Scholastic. He is also the author of *Promises To Come* (General) and *Torn Away* (Viking).